PRAISE FOR THE TIDE SERIES

I0618076

"Mesmerising. T.M. Bashford is my new favorite author. Her writing is the whole package: dynamic, well developed characters; riveting, fast moving, action packed storyline; emotionally overwhelming and heart-stopping vocabulary and language and the developing, death defying suspense makes you unable to put her book down." *Amazon Reviewer*

"I always love finding new authors, and this author is one to watch, because she has serious talent!" *Amazon Reviewer*

"It's so refreshing to read about a strong, yet realistic and complex female character." *Goodreads Reviewer*

"Drew had my heart from the beginning, but this [final] book sealed the deal." *Makala Williams, Yours Truly Book Services*

"Wow. This is definitely a 5-star read. Lots of action. Broken and unique characters." *Amazon Reviewer*

"Nothing I write in my review would ever give this book the justice it deserves." *Amazon Reviewer*

"TM Bashford shows her love of words with her intense story." *Amazon Reviewer.*

"I truly Love this story and it will forever be in my heart. Such talented writing." *Goodreads Reviewer*

"Couldn't put it down! Adrenaline and strife kept me turning the pages." *Amazon Reviewer.*

"Gripping must read!" *Amazon Reviewer*

ALSO BY T.M. BASHFORD

The Tide Series

The Heartless Tide
The Forbidden Tide
The Chilling Tide

Novella
Becoming Sienna

THE
CHILLING
TIDE

T. M. BASHFORD

THE CHILLING TIDE

Print: ISBN-13: 978-0-6486780-4-5

Digital ISBN-13: 978-0-6486780-5-2

Cover Design: Blue Water Books

Editor: Silvia Curry

Library of Congress Control Number: 2020900296

A catalogue record for this work is available from the National Library of Australia

For all of you who continue to believe in true love.

SHAE

My heart slips.

I tug my gaze from Drew toward the empty gray horizon. This time, I can't find solace in the gentle rise and fall of *Ariel* or the slap of the shifting waves against her hull. Drew's still on his knees in the cockpit, the diamond ring between his thumb and index finger. The tension in the air stretches, making it too thin to breathe.

Marry Drew? He's asking me to marry him after I ran from the life of being a rich man's girlfriend. How can he think becoming a billionaire's *wife* is any better?

Glancing back at him, Drew's eyes soak me in tenderness. But then he frowns at my hesitation, at how I blink away the treacherous tears and jerk my face up to the clouds that tumble across the cobalt sky.

He leans onto his haunches, knees planted on the damp deck. The apple he'd dropped rolls across the cockpit as *Ariel* pitches and lolls. Disappointment stumbles across his features like the tumbling clouds. I steady myself on the bench seat, hunting for the right thing to say.

"I'm sorry. I don't mean to hurt you." My words swirl,

sour in my mouth. "I just can't give you an answer right now."

His gaze slopes to my face. "Can you not forgive me? Are you still angry about Ava, even after I explained what happened?" He slips the ring into his shorts pocket, his expression bland but his eyes spinning with hurt.

"It's not that I don't..." I cannot say the 'L-word'. Not yet. "I've tried to hate you and that'll never be possible."

He captures me to him again, squeezing me. My relieved laugh sounds strangled.

"This isn't how I planned to propose," he says into my hair. "I understand we're young, but how else can I convince you that I love you? I'm sorry I hurt you. I need you to know you're my future... my everything." He chuckles. "I sound as if I'm reciting song lyrics, but I mean every word."

I let myself sink against him, savoring being held after two months of missing him so badly that some days I thought I would break into pieces. A sensation of calm washes through me, like when you come home after a very long, difficult journey. But that's not a reason to marry someone. I lay my head on his shoulder, then speak into his neck.

"I need some time with the idea. It's too much now. To be honest, I only came to find you out of guilt—it was my fault you and my brother were in danger. For weeks, I thought you were with Ava."

Drew pulls away. "Would you have come if Finn wasn't with me?"

The question takes me off-guard, but of course, I would've. "Yes."

"You hesitated."

"I hadn't thought about it before."

"But now you know the truth. I was never with Ava."

I scramble to find words to fill the silence. "I never thought marriage would be for me—not ever. I'm only twenty-four. I haven't even finished college. Or got a real job. We're two boats lost out here in a cyclone belt—with a kidnapper. *Karma* is de-masted and taking on water, and we're ninety miles from Samoa and safety. It's such a tenuous situation. We're not out of danger yet. And... and I imagined my future sailing around the world on *Sassy Jam*—I want to set a world record—and now you're here again. It's a lot..."

My next words are lodged in my throat; I can't say the final truth—that I'm not someone who can fit into his new life of red-carpet movie premieres and business lunches. And I hate the media attention that comes with being a Vega because I've always needed an invisibility cloak. He doesn't seem to realize that, which makes me wonder how well he knows me.

"As long as you feel something for me, it's enough." His tone is warm, his breath soft in my ear. "We're in a crazy situation at the moment, but whether it's next month or next year, I'm ready to marry you whenever you're ready. I just want you to know."

When he turns to kiss my forehead, I lower my gaze and stoop to pick up the green apple that's rolling across the floor. It has one bite taken from it. "Hungry, were you?"

Drew takes the apple, thrusts it into a pocket. "It kept me going. Don't laugh, but the smell of it made me feel closer to you. Remember the apple shampoo you used on *Sassy Jam*? I've turned into a lovesick, apple-smelling fool."

He rubs his thumbs over the blisters on my hands from the rope work then strokes my cheek. I make myself remember to breathe while longing to run my fingers through his milky tea-colored hair. The betrayal and jealousy which had overwhelmed me when I watched Ava with him is siphoned away by the love I sense in his touch—it soaks through my skin and into my veins like ink through water.

His face moves closer and I zero in on his mouth, which turns soft and serious. Hot, needy desire waterfalls through me. Our breaths hitch and my rabbiting heart throbs against my chest. But if we kiss or become intimate, he'll think we have a future. It'll give him the wrong signal. Instead, I drop back onto the bench seat and tap the place beside me. I glance away from his frown, pondering *Karma* bobbing quietly next to us, and then make conversation by talking about the last few weeks.

Finn, Sienna, and the other girl had thoughtfully gone below deck on *Karma*. Drew and I eventually jump across from *Ariel* and descend the companionway stairs into the cockpit to join them. The stench of wet wood is strong.

Finn is seated at a spacious dining table with his arm around Sienna. He cheers the loudest when he sees us and comes over to hug me.

"You two got things sorted, sis?" he asks. Under his dark fringe, his eyes dart between me and Drew.

Drew looks at his feet.

Suddenly embarrassed, I inspect the cabin and pray that Drew doesn't say anything about proposing to me. "This is quite a boat," I say. *Karma's* modern wooden cabin is huge. The kitchen is the same size as *Sassy Jam's* entire below deck. "Seems undamaged in here—not so good up top. What's the situation, apart from losing your mast?"

"No electrics, therefore, no equipment or lights. The bilge pump doesn't work and we're taking on water." Finn crosses his arms and clutches each shoulder before continuing, "Lost the buckets at sea when we were using them as drogues, no almanacs for the sextant, the dinghy is gone, running out of food and water. Other than that, we're pretty perfect."

"The rescue authorities have your location from the EPIRB you set off, but they held off coming out because of a cyclone threat," I say.

"And that's when you decided to mount your own rescue mission?" Drew says, his face crawling with both disapproval and admiration.

4

I shrug. "Couldn't drag you across the Pacific again and not come and help when you needed me, could I?" He pulls me to him again.

"What are we going to do?" Sienna asks. Her usually tranquil expression is pinched with worry, though she still resembles a delicate fairy from a children's storybook with her dark pixie haircut and waiflike body.

"We can always eat Eddie if we get really hungry," the girl I met in Auckland jokes. Everyone laughs. "Remember me? Colbie? We met in New Zealand?" She extends a hand but then changes her mind and engulfs me in an enthusiastic hug. "Glad we finally found you—or did you find us? Drew's been a nightmare to live with. Mooning around, staring at the stars, and sniffing apples instead of eating them. Hopefully, he'll ease up now." She darts a cheeky grin at him, her wide smile bright against her tanned skin.

"Actually, I think Eddie's more of a nightmare to live with," Drew says.

"Where is he?" I ask, eyeing the area.

"Locked in his cabin," Sienna says. Everyone stares at the door with a large hole in it. "Don't worry, he's not only tied up, but the boys secured him on the bed, which will stop him from rolling off and kicking in the door."

I glance nervously at Drew. He stares out of a porthole.

"My life feels like a movie," Sienna murmurs. "I'm starting to long for the quiet of my parents' home in Cape Cod."

"Can your boat tow us to Samoa, Shae?" Colbie asks as she munches noisily on a celery stick and twirls her blonde ponytail.

Finn grunts, skeptical. "I'm guessing you've got no communications on *Ariel*?" I shake my head. "Don't know about towing—read how to do it but never done it." Finn plunks next to Sienna at the table.

I join them, followed by Drew and Colbie. Drew lays a

warm palm on my leg. I relish the sensation of hot ripples of desire diving through my belly.

He still gets to me... in a big way.

Finn drums his fingers on the table. "I doubt we've got a line long enough for towing—or strong enough. It would need to be three hundred feet and double braided nylon at the very least. I doubt *Ariel*'s motor is powerful enough to pull us given the ocean's not exactly calm. It'd be like spinning car tires for hours on end."

"Do we wait for the rescue authorities instead?" Sienna asks. "What if a storm comes in? What if they take weeks to find us? Can we all sail to Samoa in your boat, Shae?"

Colbie nearly chokes on her celery. "What about Eddie? Don't suppose there's a lock-up cabin in Shae's boat."

"No lock-up anything," I confirm.

"You've got buckets though. We can bail out the water from below more effectively." Finn's boat builder brain is whirring. "I can fix the portholes and plug any leaks. What about flares and food?"

"Yes, to buckets and flares. No to food."

"I've got it." Finn jumps up, forgetting he's sitting at a fixed dining table and he whacks his thighs. "Please tell me you have spare fuses. We're missing the engine fuse."

"Yeah, I do."

Everyone whoops and Sienna jumps up and down.

"Then *Karma* can motor back, with *Ariel* as our safety boat," Finn says. "We have plenty of fuel. If all else fails, we can jump onto *Ariel*. With or without Eddie. If it's life or death?" He stares at Colbie.

She carries on munching and shrugs, her button nose wrinkling. "Whatever."

THE SKY IS low and the color of dirty sea salt. Drew and I

head for *Karma's* cabin roof. He sits with his back to the mast and beckons me to come sit in the circle of his body.

"The sea's a bit rough to sit like that," I choke out because I don't want to mislead him. "I'm meant to be solo sailing around the world soon." I say the words to cover my rejection while I settle a foot away from him. I'm desperate to kiss him, to let myself love him, but I know I could never last in his world.

He turns a hurt expression toward Colbie, who's helming *Karma*, and then Finn, who has taken over on *Ariel*. We're sailing fifty meters apart. Sienna is tidying the kitchen and chopping vegetables to go with the tinned tuna we have for dinner.

"I'm sorry about your dad," I say in an effort to change the subject. "Do you want to talk about it?"

His chest surges. "It was a riding accident. His horse refused a hedge. They say some pieces of shiny stones spooked the horse just before he jumped."

"Were you with your dad?" He nods. "And then I go and make it worse by running off."

"As my dad would say—let's look forward rather than backward. You're here now. We finally have each other with nothing in the way."

I stiffen.

"What?" he asks. "What's wrong?"

"I hate thinking about the future. It's always... blank."

Drew shifts his position to see my face better. "Can I fill in the blank for you?" He maneuvers me so our crossed legs touch at the kneecaps, our fingers linked. Drew's glance bobs away and returns, either embarrassed or nervous. "I hope you're on the same page as me. I understand you don't want to get married yet, but I'm in a position to... support you. Wait, that sounds wrong. I mean... give us a future. You could finish your degree in Sydney, sail boats, whatever your heart desires. Or would you prefer to live in California?" His eyes are peppered with questions—and worry.

That's just the problem—we're not on the same page. Clearly, I love Drew, but nothing has changed from when I first took *Ariel* and sailed from Townsville to Sydney to say goodbye to him. I can't live the life of a billionaire's wife. Money has never been important to me. Only sailing is—it's my invisibility cloak and has been almost all my life. My gaze slips out to sea and memories of how Drew and I argued about me doing the Sydney to Hobart race reinforce my feeling that this can't work. But it's so good to be with Drew for this short time, and I don't want to bring the fight up and spoil this moment.

"What aren't you telling me?" He always busts me. "Come on, Shae, trust me."

I push out a laugh. "I'm not hiding anything. Just thinking."

"Put me out of my misery. Is moving to Sydney something you'd at least consider doing—staying with me?"

I shrug and take my hands back to fiddle with my bikini strap.

"Overwhelm me with your enthusiasm, why don't you?" His words are full of hurt but he leans in and kisses my forehead. "It's a lot to decide but… think on it for a bit."

He doesn't move away, and I feel his breath on my skin as he speaks. A pleasant shiver passes through me.

"Break it up, you two. Time to get Finn over for dinner," Colbie yells. "Drew, can you flick the motor off?"

Dinner is a rowdy couple of hours with Finn and Drew—who are now firm friends—competing for the biggest laughs. When we're done, Finn insists on sleeping on *Ariel* in the single bunk so I can stay with Drew.

"You can have the double bed in our cabin, and Sienna and I can sleep in the bunks," Colbie says. Sienna nods in agreement though by the way she winks at Finn, I'm pretty sure she'll be joining him on *Ariel*. "I'll take first watch, too." Colbie smiles. The whole discussion turns my cheeks beetroot and I sit in my seat, wishing for that invisibility cloak. I say nothing, determined not to prolong the debate.

When everyone scatters in different directions, leaving me and Drew alone, he leads me to the cabin next to Eddie's. Inside, Drew cups my face and kisses my nose. He removes his T-shirt, and I let him lead me onto the small double bed. I'm rigid with anxiety because I'm going to have to give him my answer *now*, not after we've made love. Yet, I want him to hold me and kiss me. *Would it be wrong to do it one more time?*

"You okay? You seem tense." He pulls me next to him, his eyes brimming with love. How can I say no to someone who looks at me like that? Someone who clearly loves me. In answer, my fingertips curl through the smattering of hair on his pecs. My body is stretched with need and this feels so right, it's as if my heart is woven with his. His breathing quickens and deepens, and we turn to each other. Our desire takes over; hands race under my shirt and our mouths grab at each other, a lightning strike of passion pushing us to quickly unwrap each other until we're almost naked.

Drew groans and startles me out of my unwary state. I pull away to tell him the truth—I can't go to Sydney with him. I can't marry him. I'll never fit into the role of a rich man's wife.

There's a thud in the cabin next door and a man's voice calls out, "Got yourself a bit of hot pussy, have you, rich boy?"

I sink back onto the mattress and Drew places a finger over my lips. "Don't respond," he whispers, "it'll only make him worse." After a few moments of silence—silence which gives me time to douse the flames that burn inside me—he turns to kiss me.

"I can't," I say. "I'm too embarrassed. He's made me self-conscious—he can hear us."

Drew takes in a huge juddering breath. "Let's just be together and cuddle," he says with a smile, but the disappointment and confusion turn his smile tight.

I lie with my head on his chest and can't help but remember the times we've been intimate, but for now, I'll enjoy being in his arms. Besides, I've hardly had any sleep in two days. We can talk about the future tomorrow.

DREW

I t didn't matter that Eddie had interrupted me and Shae, or that Shae was too embarrassed to continue fooling around. I held her for hours and finally slept deeply, waking in the chalky pink light of dawn to watch her sleep. Being with her all night helped me squash the worry she'd incited in me—how she seems anxious and distant. I guess she needs time to adapt to the idea that I'm not with Ava after all. Well, we have all the time in the world.

Everyone's worried about cyclones. With no communications or radar on either boat due to water damage, we decide to motor back twenty-four-seven to halve the time it takes to reach Samoa. There's no sign of the rescue authorities—we probably missed them, having moved from the coordinates they'd be heading to.

Shae and I helm *Ariel* while Colbie and Finn take shifts on *Karma*. I steer through the sleek night while Shae is below deck catching up on sleep, which gives me time to consider our future. Before I made the crossing on *Karma* and dealt with the whole Eddie situation, I'd wracked my brain concerning who could take over *Vega Corporation* instead of me. Now, after everything we've survived, I resolve to be the one to take over the reins from my father. I know, without a doubt, if I could ask him what his final wishes were, he'd want me to head up his business. I make a deal with the universe, promising that if we arrive safely in Samoa, then I'll lead the company my father built into the future.

At three a.m., Shae emerges on deck for her watch, her espresso-colored hair blowing sexily in the wind. Desire uncoils inside me. I'm hungry to taste her, and I'm eager to feel her breath against my throat, her hands on my skin. Even though she's strong, her softness always takes me by surprise. It's as if my body was hibernating, but now it has woken up and is starving for her.

"We'll crash into *Karma* in a minute." Shae points to starboard.

I pull my eyes away from her and adjust the tiller.

"Check it out." I point into the sky where millions of stars hang like Christmas tree baubles.

"Sirius," she says, her voice dreamy.

"Finally, we're together under Sirius." I tuck her under my arm. "You smell different—not the usual apple shampoo. More roses and vanilla."

"Brett did the shopping. Guess it was his choice," she says.

Shae had explained how she helped Brett sober up and how he helped her fix *Sassy Jam*. I'm stupidly envious of the amount of time Brett has spent with Shae in the paradise of Samoa. I'm more than a little jealous that Shae got to know him—*and likes him*. I've always told her he's good at the core and is simply going off the rails because he needs professional help, but suddenly, it's her telling me how funny and clever he is, how he's changed, and can be hard-working and *sweet*. Apparently, he's determined to stay off the booze and drugs and visit a psychiatrist to finally deal with both the ordeal of being kidnapped and the feelings of abandonment he has about his father.

Although I fight a sensation of possessiveness, the subject

of Brett makes my nerves flash. He has muscled in on my girlfriends in the past, and that makes me paranoid—he's even made Shae *smell* different.

"He didn't try anything with you, did he?" I ask, remembering the night he lunged at Shae and how I had to step in.

"At first, he was a bit too... um, flirtatious."

I grip the tiller. "What? What did he do?"

She flicks her gaze out to sea and twists her T-shirt. "He was more verbally suggestive, and..."

"And what?"

"Once, he tried to kiss me. He was drunk and in a bad way when I got to Samoa, but he became open to... being helped, I guess. You gave me a second chance after you found out about Connor, and I decided to give him a second chance, too. I must've arrived on Samoa at the right moment and it wasn't difficult to persuade him off the booze. He was genuinely helpful, we had a lot of fun and he's a great cook, and he worked hard on the boat..."

"Yes, so you've said." There's something in her garbled response that makes me think she's not telling me everything. Needing to snuff out the jealousy monster, I tell myself that I trust Shae. She's probably protecting me from a truth I don't want to hear, but if she's okay, then I'm okay, too.

She starts to tell me about this great day she and Brett had kayaking, but I have to tune out to ensure the feelings of jealousy don't spark any uncalled-for anger.

THE SIGHT of Samoa looming nearer has everyone singing a medley of songs and listing the foods they're going to order the moment we get ashore. Sienna wants a margarita and a dry bed, and Colbie jokes she needs a man and a dry bed.

Shae and Finn direct us toward the Lalomanu Resort where Sienna and I worked, and I take the dinghy into shore and run to the bar to call the authorities. When they arrive, Eddie is arrested and dragged off the boat, yelling for a lawyer and making threats.

Finn smirks. "Couldn't have happened to a nicer bloke."

The four of us must give statements to the police. We talk to them one after the other and while we wait, I volunteer to treat us all to hotel rooms—the least I can do after dragging everyone through near cyclone weather and involving them in Eddie's plans to extort me. Finn calls his mom and discovers that she and Brody are already in Samoa. I insist on booking some suites in the same resort, even though Finn shares the fact that Shae's mum is furious with me for having endangered both her children's lives.

"I can't believe Mom and Brody are here," Shae says as we settle on the beach and wait for Finn's interview to finish. She scans the waves and sits a little too far from me than I'd like. "It's the Gold Coast all over again." Her face is creased with bad memories.

"No, it's not." I fling an arm around her shoulder and draw her in. "You're not about to be arrested this time." I realize she hasn't given me a final answer, even though we're now safe, to either question—moving to Sydney or marrying me.

"Got an answer for me yet about—" I can't seem to say the word.

"As an American citizen, will I be allowed to move to Sydney?" she asks.

"Not sure. You might have to marry me." I try to make the comment light, but when she smiles, there's no life in it, as if she clipped it onto her face. Her family has emigrated to Australia already, so she knows it *is* possible. Why is she stalling? Could she have fallen out of love with me? Maybe she never loved me enough? Maybe I should talk to Brett. He may provide some insight into what she's thinking now —*given they spent so much time together.*

14

I trace a finger around the edges of her hand. "I figured I'd let you and Finn go to the hotel and catch up with your family first, without me in the frame. I don't reckon I'm very popular with them... First, I made you run off because of the misunderstanding with Ava, then I take Finn on a crossing which involved kidnapping and nearly drowning at sea. I'll tackle them after you've had a family catch up and everyone is a bit more relaxed."

When Shae shrugs, I add, "I should visit Brett, too. We have a lot of unspoken things to talk through, from him attacking you in Samoa to bringing Ava and her baby to the Gold Coast. I've had a lot of time to think during the trip here, and I'd like to patch up our friendship—it's too important to me to let go. We need to clear the air so we can get back to normal when we all return to Sydney—if you decide to come to Australia..."

She says nothing. My heart feels crushed, like she has it curled in her fist. I swallow the hurt clamping my throat. "I'll meet you at the hotel afterward."

"Okay," she mumbles. "Check on *Sassy* for me, would you? And tomorrow, I must visit George."

I notice how she didn't say 'we' must visit George.

———

AFTER GETTING a taxi to George's cottage, and finding him not home, I walk along the shoreline to find *Sassy* and Brett as per Shae's instructions. The sight of *Sassy Jam* kicks at my gut. Even though Shae and I nearly died on her, those days had somehow been uncomplicated. But the sight of Brett propped in *Sassy*'s cockpit is incongruous. I stop in my tracks. I've never seen him on a sailboat, never mind peacefully staring off into the horizon. He usually can't sit still for more than a minute. More importantly, it's as if he's trespassing.

I let the unfamiliar surge of jealousy dwindle before I shout his name.

He turns and stands. "*Drew!* Friggin' hell. Where's Shae?"

"She's safe. We're all fine." I stride into the waves and dive in. After he helps me aboard, we backslap and flop on opposite bench seats to rake over each other. I decide he's sober.

I break the silence. "You're never this quiet—and calm—mate." Brett always has a joke or a story on his lips—he hates silence. "Shae said you'd changed, but I hadn't expected such a transformation."

"How did she find you? What happened?"

I explain about Eddie, how we motored back and then endured the police interviews. I also tell him I missed him at my father's funeral—which is the truth. He was there for my mother's funeral, and despite what had happened recently, he's been like a brother to me.

"Where's Shae?" he asks.

I bare my soul and he wants to know where my girlfriend is...?

"She's gone to meet up with her family. I'll brave them later," I explain. "I'm not their favorite son-in-law at the moment."

"Son-in-law?" He jumps to his feet. "What the hell are you talking about?"

Brett's definitely not right. He never lets on when he's caught off guard and he turns everything into a joke, but now he's practically snarling at me. His overly long fringe hangs across his dark eyes and makes his chin seem more pointed. He hasn't shaved either, which is a sign of trouble—yet he's not drunk or high.

"Why so serious, mate? I'm kidding. Well, half kidding. I did ask Shae to marry me." I witness that bomb drop and his reaction is unusual—he straightens, bulges his cheeks, and scans the horizon.

He doesn't look at me when he asks, "Shae's forgiven you?"

Where's the loud, love-the-spotlight Brett? Where's his usual exuberance and playful manner? I'm thrown by his stern and sensible demeanor. I choose a new topic. "I hear you helped fix up *Sassy* and you're off the booze. Shae says you're planning to go to uni..." Given his mood, I'm not sure whether to go on because visiting a psychiatrist was always a prickly subject. "And you're going to find some professional help."

The whole time I'm talking he's combing the beach, seeming as if he's expecting someone to materialize. Unease prickles up my spine.

"When are you getting married?" His Adam's apple bobs down then up.

"Not sure. Her reaction wasn't what I expected."

Brett fails to hide a glint of triumph. "She said no?" He sits down again, leaning toward me.

I shove my hand into my pocket but remember I stored the ring in a waterproof bag on *Ariel*. The apple is still there though. I take it out and place it on the bench seat. Studying Brett, I consider my next words carefully.

"She didn't say yes or no." I try to understand why that might be, but I don't have any idea what's going on in Shae's head. "I thought she was waiting until we got ashore safely before giving me an answer, but she's not said anything," I tell Brett, hoping he has some insight. "She hasn't even said anything about simply *moving* to Sydney. She knows I can't move to the States with *Vega Corp* to run. I'm starting to suspect she's not on the same page as me."

A stab of something dark tightens my stomach.

Brett's expression loosens but quickly steels up. "What did she say?" He rubs the thick stubble on his chin.

"A bunch of stuff about being too young, marriage not being for her, and wanting to be safe first."

Brett abruptly stands and the boat rocks. He turns his back to me. I'd give anything to see his face. Something is off.

Did Shae hide something from me? I remember how I had an instinct that she wasn't telling me everything.

"What's going on, Brett? Did she let on how she feels about me?"

When he swings around again, his lips are pursed. "She thought you two were over," he says. My heart cringes. "We both did."

I work to keep my expression blank, fighting the growing hollow inside me while I wait for his next words.

"I'm sorry, mate. I really am."

My stomach recoils. I rush to my feet. "What the hell are you talking about?"

"Look around you, mate. Shae and I have been living together in this sultry paradise for three weeks. We've got to know each other... intimately." He raises those stupid arched eyebrows with a smirk on his face. I want to punch it off.

"What happened?" I demand.

"Jeez, Drew, you're not one to kiss and tell. You can't ask me—"

He stops when I thump the edge of the dodger. Pain shoots up my arm. I spin to him, my jaw set. My head is on fire.

His hands go up in surrender. "This isn't easy to hear, mate. But you must understand, we both believed it was over between you. We didn't think we were doing anything wrong. You were with Ava again and we were here, living side by side, helping each other. We needed each other. She was trying to get over you and I was drying out. We worked on *Sassy*, we spent days swimming and talking, nights cozied up in the cockpit... it just happened."

Red-hot fury swims up from my feet through my belly and into my brain. "No way! I don't believe you." But I recall how Shae had raved over Brett's change, and how she said he was helpful and fun to be with. How she was uncomfortable and cagey when I asked if he tried anything with her.

18

She was definitely hiding *something*. "But you're not her type."

"*Wasn't* her type. She changed me. I'm a different person —thanks to the love of a good woman. No more booze, no drugs or parties, no misdemeanors—smell my breath." He leans in and blows air at me. "She fell for the new and improved Brett."

"Jeez, Brett. Do you realize what you're doing to me?"

"But I didn't do anything wrong, mate. You two were done."

"I can't believe this—" The way Shae acted on the boat now makes more sense. I was confused and a little hurt with how she had avoided any intimacy, not even wanting to cuddle when we sat on *Karma's* roof that first night. But would she really fall for Brett? "*No!* You always liked her—or wanted her because you knew I liked her. So, you stepped in the first chance you got. But she can't be into you, she just can't."

He sits near the tiller to put some space between us. "Why'd she say no to marrying you?"

"She didn't exactly say no." But he has a point. She didn't exactly seem excited by my proposal. Was she trying to hint at something? Had she been afraid to tell me about her and Brett?

"But she didn't say yes, either," Brett says. "She's thinking, right? Choosing between us? If she loves you, why does she need to think about it?"

I kick the bench seat, wishing I had room to pace. The memory of how Shae was unable to look me in the eye when I proposed, or even when I mentioned a future together, ghosts through my mind. Her hair didn't even smell like apples anymore, but of the shampoo *Brett* bought for her. Had I missed all her signals and coerced her into considering my view of our future? "But she came to rescue me. She risked her life to find me—"

"And her *brother*. She risked her life to save you both. When she heard the news, she accepted it was her fault. She wasn't going to leave you both out there to die. She didn't come because she loves you… she came out of guilt."

I want to unhear his words because they echo what Shae had said—and she'd hesitated when I asked her if she would have risked her life if Finn wasn't with me.

Thoughts are stuffed so tightly in my brain that it's impossible to pick them apart or make sense of anything. I slump onto the bench seat remembering how Shae had tensed when I mentioned our future, how she became unresponsive and glum when we talked about how I could create a life for us, how she hadn't exactly jumped at the idea of moving to Sydney. Instead, she brought up stupid stuff like visas—avoiding the question. Why had I ignored all her signals?

"You believe she didn't give me an answer because she loves *you*?" My throat constricts around the words.

Brett pushes long fingers through his dark hair. "She doesn't want to marry you or she'd have said yes—even if it was for a date in the far future. She made love with me and told me she loves me. She told me she could never, ever forgive you because she gave you her trust and you *betrayed* her. I was there for her when she needed someone and that counts for a lot. I wanted to come when she left to find you and Finn, but she begged me not to—said she'd die if something happened to me. She asked me to wait here and then we'd start our life together. You can't blame her, mate, can you? She moved on. She thought you had, too."

Even though she sang Brett's praises and spent a lot of time with him, even though she may have changed him and helped him, even though it did seem as if Brett was waiting for her when I arrived… it just can't be true.

She never told me she loves me, not even during our days on Sassy Jam. Is Brett right? Does Shae not love me?

"Why didn't she tell me about you?" I demand. "Why did she keep up the pretense?" I can feel the heat in my face as my lips curl around the ugly words. "Why did she lie to me?"

"Come on, mate. She spent the first week you met saying her name was Emily, and she lied about why she was on the run from California, remember? I'm not sure you understand her as well as you think you do."

I dry wash my face, wading through thoughts and memories.

"After what happened with her dad and Connor, don't you reckon she'd be cautious about telling you the truth when she was stranded on a boat with you—with no getting away from you if you went off at her?"

I stand again, speaking through gritted teeth, "She knows I'd never do that."

"But this is different. She's never had to tell you she doesn't love you anymore, that she's fallen for your *best friend*. Right now, *I'm* bloody frightened about your reaction, so why wouldn't she?" His sudden smile is criss-crossed with pity.

I grip my jaw and climb onto the gunwale.

"Where are you going?" he asks.

"To talk to Shae."

"There's no point. Shae and I leave in two days—we're going to live in California. I'm moving there right after I talk my dad into sending me to college in LA. He'll be happy I've returned to college and he'll cough up the cash. Shae's teaching me to sail. I'm buying her a boat. It's all settled, mate. She needs to sail and set world records. She doesn't want to be a businessman's wife stuck inside a mansion in a city. You have to let her go."

I put together the pieces of the puzzle. Aside from being lukewarm around the question about coming to Sydney, she'd repeatedly mentioned Brett with a sparkle in her eyes, and she'd brought up the idea of breaking sailing world records twice. I know how sailing is a part of her soul. Yet, if it wasn't for Eddie yelling and listening in, we would've had sex. Everyone had assumed we'd share a cabin, including myself. Had she been bulldozed into sleeping with me? Or was it to be goodbye sex? Is that why she didn't want to have sex and used Eddie as the excuse? Even hours after he'd called out to us, she wasn't interested. At one point, I'm sure she pretended to be asleep. It's ironic how she has major trust issues, yet she's the best liar I've ever met. Brett's right on that point.

"Brett, you're not the most trustworthy when it comes to—"

"I've got something to show you." Brett beckons me down from the gunwale. "It's concrete proof about what I'm telling you. This is not just words."

I acquiesce and follow him into the cabin. At the nav table, he pulls out a plastic file. I recognize the drawings immediately—the sketches I made of Shae in Samoa and when we were sailing on *Sassy Jam* toward Australia. He passes one to me. It's wrinkled, as if it'd been screwed up, with 'I'll never forgive you' scribbled across it and small holes gouged out of it. She'd stabbed the paper with a pen. The next one reads, 'It's over' in huge capitals.

My heart folds over on itself.

Brett puts a steadying hand on my shoulder, studying me through his floppy fringe. "She's done with you, Drew. She chucked these out just a few days ago, but I saved them for her. Figured she may regret it. Then when she realized you'd followed her, she had no choice but to attempt to save you and her brother if she was to live with herself. Don't put her through more than she's already been through. Allow Shae to choose her life without you *pressuring* or *guilting* her into staying with you. If you love her as you say you do, then you should give her the freedom she needs without making her choose."

The sight of my vandalized sketches clarifies why Shae hesitated to discuss our future on *Karma*. She hadn't been worried about a visa or rushing into anything or getting to safety first... she delayed the discussion because she's moved on and is with Brett now. I clench my fists to stop myself from lashing out. She's not entirely to blame. She had thought we were over. And she lied to avoid telling me she'd fallen for my best friend just as she lied about Connor. That time she'd allowed us to become close, even while knowing she was going to be arrested.

"Don't make this harder on her than it already is," Brett says.

A memory of Shae's face, smiling and eyes sparkling as she re-told stories of Brett and what they'd done in Samoa, nudges me. "You went on a kayaking trip?" Shae seemed to go quiet after recalling the trip as if lost in the memory.

"She told you about that? That's when things got real hot between us."

I can't listen to what Brett has to say. Can't look at his smug face for a moment longer. Alarm bells ring in my head, knowing I'd misread her just as I had, in the past, misread Brett—and even my father. My heart caves with the realization I must let her go. I rocket onto the deck and dive into the ocean. When I reach the shore, my legs take over and I'm running along the beach in the opposite direction of town.

SHAE

When the taxi drops me off in the parking lot, I don't wait for my change but run onto the beach. *Sassy Jam* is where I last saw her, forlorn without her mast. Apart from the fact that someone's lit the lanterns, there's no sign of Drew or Brett.

I stand on the shoreline and yell their names. It's been four hours and I was impatient for Drew to return to the hotel given Finn was slurring his words and acting obnoxious after several beers and Mom hadn't stopped lecturing me. Apparently, it's time to stop sailing to wherever I fancied, stop taking stupid risks, and stop putting people in danger. Brody stayed silent—maybe he agrees with her.

It's possible Brett and Drew went to a bar for a drink to celebrate. I hope Brett sticks to OJ.

I smile with relief when Brett emerges. He waves and beckons to me. I pull my T-shirt over my head, remove my shorts, leaving them on the sand, and swim to *Sassy*. I trace my fingers over her raspberry-red letters, happy to be home.

"I should be bloody angry with you for abandoning me," Brett says, his expression anything but angry. He helps hike me onboard.

"I did not abandon you." He hugs me for a little too long and I have to pull away. "Where's Drew?" I glance into the cabin but it's quiet and dim. Brett passes me a towel, his sharp jaw suddenly set. His bitter chocolate eyes avoid me. Dread quivers through me like a vibrating guitar string. "Where's Drew?" I repeat.

"Sit," Brett says as he bumps down onto the bench seat. When he doesn't speak and won't look at me, I blink at the filthy dishwater-colored sky and take in a deep breath.

"Where is he, Brett? Did you two argue? Tell me." Panic takes over and a gush of heat throbs through my skull. For a moment, I wonder if Brett has found where I hid the gun on *Ariel*.

Brett leans on his knees and holds his head in his hands. "He's gone."

"Gone? Gone where? Why?" Frantic, I push at his shoulder to make him look at me. "Tell me, Brett."

"He told me he asked you to marry him?" I nod, remaining confused. "But you said no?"

"Not exactly, but why does that matter?"

"You've got to understand, Shae... he's a different person now."

"Different? How different? You're not making any sense."

"He was angry. No, not angry. Put off? Hurt? I think it hurt him but mostly, he seemed... offended?"

My mouth pops open. There are no words but there's a jungle-drum beat in my chest.

"That's what I mean—he's not the same Drew as we knew. He's a billionaire, Shae. He's not like us anymore. He's the kind of guy who gets kidnapped for a ransom. He's the kind of guy who can have whatever he wants—including any woman. Then there's you saying you're too young or something. I reckon he needed you to be completely ecstatic and impatient to be his wife."

I try to stand, but my legs won't support me. "What did he say exactly? Word for word."

"Just—jeez I'm sorry, Shae." His cupid's bow lips purse together.

He comes over to comfort me, but I pull my legs to me and push him away. "Tell me."

"Something similar to, 'If she won't marry me, plenty of other women will.'"

"*No.* He wouldn't say that."

"You're thinking of the old Drew. The one from a few months ago. He's inherited everything from his father—he's one of the richest and most powerful men in Australia, the world, even. You don't think that's going to change him? Look at what happened with Ava—he could have refused to even let her in the house if he meant what he said about her being out of his life. She had recently tried to trick him into being a father to her baby. He has a guard to keep people he doesn't want to see out. Clearly, he was happy to accept her visit."

Brett's words echo my thoughts before I ran away on *Ariel.* Drew had changed to me, too—flying in private jets, and dressed in suits and leather Armani shoes rather than swimmers and being barefoot. Isn't that why I had gone to Sydney in the first place—to tell him I couldn't fit into his new life and had decided to carry on sailing? Now, Drew's not the son of a wealthy man, but a billionaire in his own right. Merely a couple of days ago, my heart had woven together with Drew's but today it's tearing at the seams.

"Look how much *I've* changed in barely three weeks," Brett adds. "Drew's changed, too. I noticed it immediately. He has this air of entitlement. I guess that's natural when everyone around you jumps at your every command. When you can buy anything you want in the world. When you have power. Power and money changes people."

26

Connor had had both power and money. But this is Drew, not Connor. "What else did he say?"

"He was glad to get off the boat, that it was hard to be with you when you'd rejected him. His new ego couldn't take it. He said something about you stringing him along and how Ava would never do that. He's returning to Sydney as soon as possible. Tonight, even."

Is that why he hadn't come to the hotel with me? It had seemed slightly odd that he chose to visit Brett instead of staying with me to face the music with Mom and Brody. I struggle to recall his reaction when I couldn't answer his proposal and I remember the confusion there, but maybe there was some surprise, too. Had the expression that crossed his features before he turned away been annoyance rather than hurt?

I shove my head into my knees and a scary wail pushes out of me. Brett sits next to me and this time, I let him hold me. Ugly, guttural gasps wrack through me. Brett rocks me against his bear-like body and brushes his palms up and down my arms until the sky turns to charcoal and begins to spit.

As I ponder the endless heavens, the raindrops sparkle like tiny falling gems in the moonlight.

"Jeez," I finally say, "the world is crying."

The rain turns torrential and Brett helps me into *Ariel's* cabin. He finds another towel, wraps me in it, and sits me on the edge of the bunk. When he goes to boil the kettle to make hot chocolate, a sharp sense of loss spikes through me. I hold myself across the stomach, as if I've been cut in half. That's when I spot the apple, discarded on the nav station just as Drew had discarded me—the lone bite mark turning brown.

"Why didn't you agree to marry him?" Brett's words split the silence in two.

I blink at him. Shut my eyes. Open them again.

"I'm not who he thinks I am," I say, my voice stretched and scratchy.

Brett ambles toward me. He slumps to his knees, his face level with mine. I flip onto my belly. He places a flat palm on my back. "You've had a lucky escape, then." His palm rubs circles over my shirt.

I stare at the discarded apple on the nav table.

"I'm here for you, Shae," he adds and strokes my hair. "I won't leave you."

"There can be nothing between us, Brett, not even now."

"I'll simply be the best friend you need."

"But you'll never give up, will you?"

He's quiet for a while, coaxing the ends of my hair through his fingers like a loom. "No. *I'll* never give up on you. Never stop loving you. Never stop hoping. No matter what you say."

I don't respond. What is there to say? I'll be leaving soon and will probably never see him again.

"Are you still planning to sail around the world?" he asks.

"Yes. But I need to do it properly. I was rushing into it. Brody made me see that. *Ariel* doesn't even have the right communication equipment. I'm going to return to California where I have a lot of yachting friends and my father's old contacts at the yacht club. They'll help me raise the funds I need."

I had considered returning to Townsville, but it hadn't worked out last time with Mom fussing over me and pressuring me to buckle down and stop sailing.

"You're going to California?" Brett asks.

"Yes." I grit my teeth. "Soon." I won't stay in Samoa any longer. Not with reminders of Drew everywhere. "My family return to Townsville in two days. Brody and Finn plan to sail *Ariel* back. Apparently, she's not safe for anyone to solo sail at the moment. They can do repairs along the way."

"Then I'm coming with you." His voice is strident.

"*No*, Brett. You're returning to Sydney to start your life, to find professional help, to get your life on the right track."

"I can do that in California. I'm not leaving you after what's happened. We helped each other before, we can do it again. I promise I won't drink, and if I do, you can banish me forever. I'm not expecting anything romantically, but I won't be talked out of being your friend. Don't even try. I'll book us some flights in the morning."

Remembering the night when he put the gun to his temple makes my stomach contract. But it's not as if I can stop him from flying to California. When we arrive, I can distance myself from him. He'll meet someone else to distract him. Besides, right now, I don't have any fight left in me.

I inspect *Sassy Jam*. Despite all our work, she's not even close to seaworthy. It's just one more goodbye to come.

DREW

J amison stands in the doorway in a full suit and tie. His lined face fights not to break apart. "Mr. Vega, thank the heavens. It's..."

"I'm sorry, Jamison. I understand how much you must have worried."

"Yes, sir. A trying time. But you've returned safely." He searches behind me, his thin lips taut. I step into the hallway, and he peeks outside again before shutting the door.

"Yes, I'm alone, Jamison," I say.

"Miss Love? She's safe?"

"Yes. She's fine. But we're done. It's over." It takes every ounce of iron will to keep my expression set, to stop it from crumpling. I rub the skin between my eyebrows. "We both must move on with our lives."

Jamison, standing ramrod straight, browses over me, his thoughts and emotions hidden behind his 'butler face'.

"Very well, sir." He picks up the holdall I'd discarded. "Will it be tea in the kitchen or your room?"

"I need a shower... and some sleep." I walk across the hall and glance at the closed double doors of Dad's study. I have no one now, not even Brett.

I begin the climb up the stairs. "One last thing, Jamison." I take the bag from him and find his pale eyes are watery. "Keep Ava Andrews away from me. I never want to see her again." My voice sounds like someone else's—someone hard and unemotional. I sound similar to my father before we reunited.

In my bedroom, I observe the expertly made bed in the center. The suit I wore to Dad's funeral—barely a month ago—hangs on the closet door, a dry cleaner's plastic bag protecting it. Through the double doors leading to the balcony, the sky is the color of an old bar of soap.

After leaving Brett on *Sassy*, I had run up the beach for miles before finding a taxi to take me to the airport. There, I booked the next flight out, not caring where it took me. Samoa was supposed to be paradise, but it had taken Shae from me and I couldn't stay there a minute longer. The journey took me via Papua New Guinea, where I dozed in an uncomfortable chair before catching the next flight to Sydney.

Craving a shower, the mirrors reflect my movement toward the bathroom. I expect to see the shadows under my eyes, the stubble, how pale I am, but I don't expect to see the eyes that stare back at me—empty and dead.

OVER THE FOLLOWING WEEKS, I shadow Dad's colleagues—my colleagues—appoint a mentor, and devour company documents and news clippings. If I'm to take over Dad's empire, I need to learn fast. I consider getting an art degree on the side but every time I do, I'm walloped by the memory of the sketches Shae had scribbled over, crumpled and discarded. I can't draw any more.

I'm in the gym each day at six. The punching bag gets a pasting, then I'm off to the office for business meetings and company training, rarely returning before eight for dinner. After that, there's more document reading and a final boxing session before I lay in bed, battling to sleep. Tonight, I give up on getting any shuteye at three a.m. and read some notes I made during an earlier meeting. There's a soft tap on my door. Jamison pokes his head into the room.

"I saw the light on," he says, "and I took the liberty of making you some tea." His bushy eyebrows are pushed up like question marks.

I'd barely spent any time with Jamison since my return and hadn't indulged in any kitchen visits to talk with a pot of tea between us. I suppose I'm avoiding a discussion about what had happened because it hurts, and I can't form the words. Instead, Jamison hovers nearby, and I've kept myself occupied. I expect he's waited in the kitchen late into the night, hoping I'd come for tea and sandwiches or hot chocolate and chocolate chip cookies as I had in the past.

A ripple of guilt makes me swing my legs out of bed. "Thanks, Jamison. Come in."

"I took the liberty of making one for myself, too." He marches over to the table and chairs by the window, settles the tray, and begins to pour, his back as straight as if there's a wooden plank permanently fitted to the inside of his suit jacket. I pull on a dressing gown.

"Working?" he asks. "I'm afraid you're turning into your father."

I don't know how to reply. I had avoided becoming like my dad for most of my life, but I learned too late that he was a great man. He believed in what he was building, built businesses which benefited society, and sent profits to countries in need. He wasn't the stone-hearted, hard-nosed capitalist I had thought him to be. I had always criticized him for the lack of balance he had in his life—especially after Mom died. He had left Jamison to father me and I'd resented that, even though Jamison is as dear to me as any father.

But *I* have no one to disappoint if I work twenty-four hours a day. No one is going to miss me.

I sit and take a sip of tea. "Is mimicking Dad such a bad thing? As he did, I'm discovering the job is a good distraction."

Jamison sits deep into his chair, unbuttons his suit jacket, and crosses his legs. "It depends on your reasons, though. He was building something—creating jobs, providing for you and your mother. He loved everything he did. It was a hobby, therefore working all those hours the day delivered wasn't a chore."

I shrug, dismissing the hint.

"But you toil away like it's a punishment," he adds.

"I've got a lot to learn in a short amount of time." My gaze settles on Jamison's concerned face. "I've got a lot to prove... a lot to live up to."

"Your father didn't become the man he was overnight—and certainly not at the age of twenty-four."

I nod in acknowledgment.

"Miss Love? Is the *Vega Corporation* helping to distract you from a broken heart?"

I put the teacup on the saucer and spin it around. "I'll get there, Jamison. For now, this is working for me."

Jamison sips his tea and I get up and open the French doors to let in some night air. I'm tortured by the sight of Sirius.

"How are you finding everything at the office?" he asks. "Are your colleagues helpful? Professional?"

"Yes, they are. It's coming together. The hardest part is the hate mail. People tarnish every rich man with the same brush, believing him to be greedy, heartless, and hard-nosed. They hate me because I'm wealthy. Someone even made a death threat because they think our company is supporting terrorists and as I'm head of the company... it's just not true. I didn't expect any of that."

"I assume the police have been informed."

"There's a whole company process we follow. It's not the first time this has happened."

"Perhaps that's why your father had this estate secured and a guard stationed at the gate. Arnold, your driver, is ex-FBI."

"He is? Great." I don't mention it to Jamison, but I worry about backlash from Eddie. What if he's after revenge and this is a way of getting it? I inspect the high brick walls covered in vines that surround the house. "Then there's the trickle of letters from people claiming that they're the love-child of my dad and they should inherit his estate."

"It proves the average person can be as greedy and unscrupulous as the clichéd image of a wealthy businessman. Except these members of the public are lazy, too—attempting to make money without working for it."

"I'm a target, Jamison, a lone fish in a pool with people throwing spears at me, wanting me gone for no explicit reason. How did my father live with that?"

"I suppose he focused on all the good he was doing."

Not for the first time, I wish I'd reunited with my father sooner.

Jamison clears his throat. "Master Brett telephoned this morning." My body clenches, the breath frozen in my lungs. "He asked you to return his call."

"Thanks." *Like that's ever going to happen.* The silence is long, and Jamison takes his cue and tidies the tray.

"Night then, Drew." I cut to him. His expression is charged with double-meanings—sympathy, confusion, sorrow, fondness. He's never called me anything other than Master Drew and since Dad's death, it's either sir or Mr. Vega. We've argued about it; I always hated the formality of it —how it made me feel like he was a servant when he is closer to an uncle.

"Night, Jamison."

He balances the tray and leaves the room.

"Jamison," I call. He opens the door again, his wayward eyebrows pushed up. "If Brett should phone again, please tell him I'm out—no matter what." Jamison strains to keep his expression blank. He's entertained Brett with cookies and hot chocolate since Brett and I first became friends twenty years ago.

To: Drew dvega@thevegacorporation.com
   From: Brett dreamlover12@yahoo.com
   Subject: Checking in

HEY MATE,

I hope you're okay. Jamison said you're fine. Can't seem to reach you by phone. You're probably screening my calls. I understand you're angry, but please remember we both thought it was over between you.

We've moved to California. Shae's finishing college then plans to solo sail around the world. Not sure how I'll cope with her leaving, but that's a year away—it's not the easiest thing to organize. She's fine, by the way. I know you worry about her.

My parents have agreed to enroll me at UCLA as long as I study law. Whatever, eh?

Guess you're pretty busy taking over your new empire. Have fun with that. Don't forget us little people.

BRETT (who still sees himself as your best mate if you need one)

SHAE

Having spent most of the last five months either on a boat or in Samoa, I wonder if returning to the crowded, traffic-ridden California is another bad decision. I long to wake on *Sassy* instead of the small room I rent in West Hollywood from Emily, my old college roommate, where sirens, car horns, and loud voices are a constant backdrop. Emily graduated and lives alone after a recent break up with a boyfriend.

Despite living in a city with a population of millions, I need my invisibility cloak more than ever. I'm the girl who killed her partner, and people are either impressed and slap me on the shoulder or they are wary and whisper behind their hands.

"I assumed guys would be more mature once they left college," Emily says. We're both carrying grocery bags up the hill to the apartment. "But they're just as bad. I might have to target the over thirties to find someone half decent who isn't playing the field." She blows irritably at her blunt cut bangs, her blond bob swaying around her cheeks.

My mind wanders to *Sassy*. Before I left Samoa, I visited George to ask him to tow her to his jetty, but his cottage was locked up. I waited for two hours before leaving a note in his mailbox suggesting *Sassy* could be his new pet project. I must call the *Coconut Palm Beach Resort* where he teaches surfing and get his phone number.

"Did you hear me?" Emily stops. She's puffing from the incline of the road.

"Sorry. I was preoccupied."

"Still moping about Drew?" She rolls her brown eyes and we continue walking. "I've survived a dozen break ups. You need to find a distraction—another guy usually works."

"Not moping. Thinking about going sailing in the Christmas break," I lie.

"You've just started teaching at your old yacht club and now you're craving a sailing holiday?"

"Teaching is different than going alone."

"Haven't you had a gutful of the ocean? Shouldn't you be moving on and making changes? Go party and replace that plate of deliciousness."

"I owe Ryan for giving me my old job, so no late-night partying for me."

Emily stops walking again. I turn to her, wondering what I've not heard this time.

"Well, *hello,* gorgeous," she says as she peeks past my shoulder.

I peer up the hill toward our apartment. Brett is marching closer and waving.

"Shit," I say under my breath. Some part of me is happy to see him. We became friends while in Samoa and shared some great times, but most of me wants him to stay away. Sometimes, I have nightmares about the time he put a gun to his head because I wouldn't kiss him or love him back, and I'm aware he's unpredictable enough for that to be repeated in some way. But he also brings out the 'fixer' in me. Despite all he's done, I worry about him. He needs help because of the kidnapping and how his father treated him. I know what it's like to have a father who makes you feel unloved. I want to fix Brett, or at the very least, help him get on the right track. I nearly succeeded in Samoa. He was a different person—the real Brett—until the kayaking day.

"Hope you don't mind me dropping by," he shouts and marches toward us. "If I wait for an invite, I might never see you. It's been at least two weeks."

Emily looks from me to Brett and back again. His pace quickens and he strides straight into me without slowing down, bear hugs me, and lifts me clear off the ground. My cheeks burn. When he plunks me down, he holds my shoulders.

"You seem okay. Functioning at least." He chuckles and takes my shopping bag. I surreptitiously sniff for alcohol and he passes the test. His expression turns from concerned parent to shunned lover. A shadow crosses his face and his eyes scald mine. "Did you miss me?" he growls.

Emily's jaw hits the pavement.

I place my lips into a smile. "This is Brett. Brett, meet my friend, Emily."

"Hey, Emily," he says, but his gaze doesn't leave my face. He's cut his hair and his bangs don't reach the tip of his nose anymore. "What Shae meant to say is 'This is Brett, my best friend in the world, the one who's always there for me and who's moved here from Australia to make sure I'm okay'… that Brett."

"I think you'll find *I'm* her best friend," Emily quips.

"We should collude then. We'll soon have the Gotta Go Girl back in the game." He finally peels his gaze from me and turns to her. "Emily? You're the girl Shae stole the name from."

Emily gives me a pointed stare. "You need to fill me in, bestie, cause I'm a bit lost here."

"When I arrived in Samoa, I was worried about being

identified so I used your name. First one that popped into my brain."

"I'm honored." Emily adjusts the bag in her arms.

"Let me take your bag," Brett says. He pulls it from her grasp without waiting for an answer and takes mine as well.

We turn toward what is now home and Brett tells us he's enrolled at UCLA and lives nearby, but in this traffic, it's an hour's car trip.

"You look too old to be a student," Emily says. "I mean that in a good way."

"Dropped out of a business degree in Australia, then went traveling. I'm trying to finish it over here. Shae and I are helping each other get our lives sorted."

"You're welcome to come over anytime," Emily says.

Brett's eyes graze over me. No wonder I prefer solo sailing—my life just got complicated again.

Despite living an hour apart, Brett visits me often, bringing magazines, curry dinners he's cooked himself, Cokes, and humorous college stories. He even whisks me to Disneyland. He's relaxed and friendly, and I enjoy his company. Maybe I can get him back on track after all. Once the holidays kick in, Emily, Brett, and I take road trips to Mexico, Vegas, and north to Sequoia National Park. Brett is nothing but charming and makes us laugh. He helps me forget my severed heart for a while. My family thinks we're getting together, and they're glad—I told them Drew chose a different life to the one I wanted, and we split up.

In my weaker moments, I Google Drew. He's a media magnet, often photographed arriving at public social events or in a box at a big football game. Sometimes he's pictured after an announcement about the *Vega Corporation*, wearing a suit and shaking someone's hand. I browse the photos, numb with confusion and longing. It's as if *we* never happened. But it always turns to anger. He's the one who gave up on me and left. *Never again.*

One day, at the end of January—two months after we left Samoa—Drew is on the front page of the yachting magazine I subscribe to. He's pictured at a Royal Sydney Yacht Squadron jetty, part of a group of men with the harbor and several yachts in the background. Apparently, Drew joined the private club late last year and is a keen crew member. As a result, he's agreed to finance Australia's challenger boat for the America's Cup.

A part of me is proud he's continued sailing. But I'm engulfed by a clogging sadness knowing we'll never sail together again.

If I'm to move forward, I need to stop delving into his world. I vow not to Google him again.

DREW

Colbie finally returned to Sydney after staying in Samoa for a holiday, and after her parents begged her to return for Christmas.

"Hello, moneybags," she says down the phone. "I had to get your number from your office and even then, I had to get approval from this guy named Jamison. How posh."

"Sorry. I'll give you my cell."

"Ooh, a direct line to the most eligible *gay* bachelor in Sydney."

"Gay bachelor?"

"Don't you read the news? Apparently, you go to parties, regattas, charity events, and award nights, but always without a date. They're speculating that you're gay."

"There are worse things they could speculate about. What else are they saying?"

"That you've joined some Royal Yacht club. Eddie didn't put you off, then?"

"No. In fact, the club's become my second home. I met this guy, Christian, and he's helped me improve my skills." When I'm sailing, my heart uncurls from the tight ball it has rolled itself into. At least for a short time, I'm calmer. It's not that I want to feel closer to Shae—I know that part of my life is over—but sailing makes me content, yet strong and in control, unlike at any other time. The yacht club saves me, and I no longer work sixteen-hour days or find reasons to work on the weekend.

"My parents have asked to meet you," Colbie adds. "I told them you're pretty dull and self-important, but they haven't let up."

"They understand we're just friends, right?"

"Course. You're too much of a good guy for me. They'd love you and we can't have that. Heard from Shae?"

"Nope."

"She still got your heart, then?"

"Yep."

"Are you ever going to tell me what happened?" she asks.

"In fifty years when it doesn't hurt to think about."

The news that I've agreed to finance the Australian challenger for the America's Cup distracts the media from my sexuality. Being involved in the race also means I meet like-minded people and travel to watch races all over Australia, New Zealand, and even Europe. Unlike my dad, it helps me achieve the balance I've always hoped to have in my life, except that I'm the loneliest man on the planet.

To: Drew dvega@thevegacorporation.com
   From: Brett dreamlover12@yahoo.com
   Subject: Life on Mars
   Hey mate,
   It's been a while. Figured I'd touch base.

   LA is pretty mad—but I embrace the madness. Americans embrace life with both hands—my kind of people. I'm absorbing the culture from Mexico to Vegas, I've met Mickey Mouse, and surfed on the equivalent of Bondi Beach.

I click on the attachment, a photo of Shae and Brett, arm in arm at Disneyland.

Uni's okay, Shae's even better. I'd say 'hi' from her, but you're a bit of a taboo subject and she doesn't talk about you. She's sailing a lot—trying to teach me—

I hit delete.

I call the IT department at my office and ask them to give me a new email address. "Cancel the old one, effective immediately."

———

"JAMISON, I've had Margaret confirm a flight out to the UK for the end of May. I'm going to the Ostar—to keep Christian company and also his family while he's sailing in the race. He's entering his Sparkman & Stephens 34."

"Excellent, sir." Jamison's beaming smile reaches the corners of his crinkling eyes. "I'll mark my diary."

"You could take some time off, maybe visit your home country?"

Jamison sucks in a breath. He pulls himself even straighter. "Absolutely not, sir. I need to be here in your absence."

"If you say so, Jamison."

"Tell me about this race. Do they have to sail once around the UK?"

"Farther than that. They set off from the south of England and cross the Atlantic to Rhode Island—it's an amateur event, not quite the America's Cup, but it attracts some serious sailing sorts."

"A bit of a jolly for you then, sir? Sounds excellent. Cup of tea?"

"Only if you have chocolate chip cookies."

He winks and beckons me to follow him into the kitchen. As we pass through the house, I glance through Dad's study doors, now permanently left open. I can't work in his space, preferring the small desk in my bedroom, but looking into the room doesn't make my gut twinge as much anymore. I miss him, but for the first time in my life, I sense he'd approve of what I'm doing—he'd approve of me.

On the way to the kitchen, I pick up an envelope lying on the hall table. It's addressed to me and I rip it open as I follow Jamison. He turns at the sound of the tearing paper.

"I had intended to forward that to your PA," he says. "We don't accept mail at the home address. Margaret should deal with any correspondence for you in the first instance."

I scan the letter, sent from a legal firm. "It's someone else claiming to be my half-brother." I crumple it. "If all those claims were true, I'd have a hundred siblings. Ever since Dad's death, it seems everyone's his son or daughter."

Before I go to bed, I unwrap a small package Jamison had placed on my desk. Earlier, he cautiously mentioned receiving it: it's from Miss Shae Love in California. What's inside hurts as much as a gunshot through the chest—the engagement ring I'd left behind on *Ariel*.

SHAE

"What's your big proposition?" I ask Ryan and take a sip of the lime and soda he just bought me. He's the boss at the club where I work, as well as a professional sailor at the Windward Yacht Club.

Ryan taps the cast on his broken leg, which is awkwardly stuck out to the side of him. "I've already got my yacht in England for the Ostar, but then this happened yesterday."

"I heard about your accident. It wasn't even due to sailing?"

"I'll never volunteer to clean out the gutters again. My wife did warn me, but... well, the rest is history."

"So, you want me to fetch your boat from Plymouth and sail her back?"

"Actually," he takes a sip of his beer and casts his gaze over the yachts below us, "I'm asking you to skipper the race."

"What? Why me?" I spill a little of my drink as I set it on the table.

"You bloody solo-sailed the Pacific in the middle of cyclone season twice. I think you can handle it. It'll be brilliant publicity for the club to have one of our staff in the race. And I've seen you sail. You're talented. You sail with your gut and not many people can do that. I want to give you this opportunity. Besides, it'll be good publicity for my boat and for you—potential sponsors for your world trip will pay attention if you do well. It's a win-win. Then you can sail her home from Rhode Island or bring her back by trailer—your choice. All expenses paid."

My soul jumps at the opportunity. Not only am I longing to solo sail again, but this time I'd experience the Atlantic and it could give me the publicity I need to raise money for my goal of sailing non-stop around the world. Mounting my campaign is slow going and raising the funds is impossibly hard. My dream won't happen if I don't do something drastic or get lucky. Brett said his family could finance my trip, but there's no way I would allow myself to be indebted to him. He might expect payment in ways I can't think about.

I wonder why Ryan hasn't asked a more experienced sailing instructor at the club. "You're sure? What about Albert?"

"Apart from the fact that he has three kids and isn't able to drop everything at a moment's notice, my sponsor has approved you. They love the fact you're young and a woman. The media will love you. Publicity is set. A shame to waste it."

"When would I need to leave?"

"Five days. It's short notice—"

"I'll do it." I put my hand out and we shake on it.

"GEORGE, IT'S ME, SHAE."

"Hey up, my little sirène. How are you? Keepin' out of mischief?"

"I came by to see you before I left Samoa, but you weren't home."

46

"What a shame. I was… working. Probably a good thing or I'd have scolded you for running off and risking your life. But I suppose it all ended well."

"I miss you, George. How's *Sassy Jam*?" I call George every couple of weeks, and sometimes sense he sits by the phone, waiting to hear from me by the way it's always snatched up.

"She's grea'. I'm enjoying tinkering on her. Needs a mast, mind you."

"Thanks for taking care of her for me. One day, I'll buy a mast. But I called to let you know I'm doing the Ostar. I wondered if you'd want to follow the race blog. I'm sailing a friend's boat named *Gambit*."

"Fantastic. Did I ever tell you I did the Ostar twenty years ago? Which route are you taking?"

"The Rhumb line."

"Ha. I took an easier option—Azores route. Wow, I'm jealous." The line is silent for a moment. "How's everything else?"

"My family returned to Townsville. Finn and Brody are building boats, and Mom's going to yoga classes. Finn and Sienna split up, though. She didn't warm to Townsville—too remote for her. Finn said she was a scaredy cat when they went sailing. He couldn't imagine having a girlfriend who hated the ocean. She's back in England."

There's a long, crackling silence before he asks, "And Brett? Do you know where he went?"

George has always scolded me for giving Brett a second chance, and I don't want to argue with him, so I don't mention Brett's moved to LA. Besides, Brett's not drinking and is managing to make a name for himself on campus for reasons other than drinking—football. He's using his size to his advantage.

Through the window, I catch sight of Brett parking his car. He appears agitated and parks badly, his rear sticking into the street. "Sorry, I have to run, George. I'll call again soon."

"Sure thing, love. Enjoy the Ostar." The line goes dead and I picture George in his cluttered cottage, surrounded by lumpy rugs, plaid armchairs, and plates of used tea bags. Outside his windows though, is the most idyllic view of the beach. *I miss him.*

"Shae! I got your message. Are you trying to give me a heart attack?" Brett bundles through the front door and collects me into a bear hug.

"Don't even try to talk me out of it." I pull free and walk toward the kitchen—Brett is an eating machine. "You know I'm mounting a world campaign. This is nothing by comparison."

"I wasn't expecting it. You have to give me time to prepare."

"It's not as if you're coming." I ignore the hurt expression on his face and open the fridge, pulling out ham and tomatoes to make him a sandwich.

"Why can't I come? I could help—"

I stop slicing the tomatoes. "No, Brett. I'm doing this alone."

Brett's reaction sweeps to anger in two seconds flat. He shoves over the bar stool. I freeze mid-slice and Brett stares at the ground. The air is heavy with tension and the walls seem to close in. He bends to pick up the stool and turns to me, his expression full of remorse.

"Sorry." His huge shoulders slump. "That was uncalled for." He reaches across and covers my hand with his, obscuring the tomato, too. The tenderness in his eyes is intense and startles me. It's been weeks of an easy friendship, and now this.

I slowly pull my hand from his grasp. "Are you visiting a psychiatrist yet, Brett? Like you promised."

"Yeah, yeah." His eyes bore into me, suddenly grave. I look away and finish making his sandwich.

When will he get the message that I will never trust anyone with my heart ever again? And when will I learn he won't ever change? It seems I resemble my mother more than I realized, staying around in the hope of fixing a man who simply can't be fixed.

DREW

Gavin Myers stares gravely at me from across his desk. He was my father's second-in-command and now acts as my mentor while I learn the ropes of Dad's empire. Without Gavin, I'd be lost.

"I'm confused," I say. "Why is this claim any more legitimate than all the others?" I peer at the legal letter he's holding, fed up with the amount of greed in this world.

"Because this claimant has gained the court's permission to have your father's body exhumed in order to complete a paternity test."

I stand, suddenly hot and needing to remove my suit jacket. "This is crazy. Can anyone decide to dig up my father?"

"Not at all. You have to go through the legal system the correct way. His claim was validated due to two things." He shakes the letter. "His birth mother is Rebecca Cunningham, a woman widely known to be an acquaintance of your father after she married into the Abspoel family."

"Wait. Abspoel? Brett's mother? Is Brett claiming he's my father's son?"

"No, not Brett. Brett's supposed half-brother, Lucas."

"Brett doesn't have a half-brother."

Gavin holds up a finger and further consults the letter. "His claim is that he's the son of Rebecca and your father. A fact less widely known is your father and Rebecca were in a relationship in their teens. Lucas is thirty-four and therefore, was born before your father met and married your mother. Ten years before Brett—or you—were born."

"That would've made my father seventeen years old when Lucas was supposedly born."

"Correct. Here's where the more compelling evidence comes in. Lucas was put up for adoption. Rebecca and your father clearly decided not to bring him up, which, given their young ages—she was sixteen—wouldn't have been uncommon. While his birth certificate does not name a father, his adoption papers were signed by both your father and Rebecca. This is the reason he was granted the order to exhume your father's body."

I begin to pace, wondering if it'd be nice to have a half-brother. "The paperwork is authentic?"

"I've yet to have everything checked out. But I decided you should know, in case—the media has a habit of digging up this sort of thing."

"It's fine. I don't care if my father had another child. He'll be family then. I don't have a lot of that. If Lucas's claim is legitimate, I'll open my arms to him."

Gavin asks me to take a seat. I do, loosening my tie.

"I'm afraid it's not so simple, Drew. If his claim is legitimate, it means Lucas is entitled to inherit your father's estate. He has as much of a right to it as you do. Everything you own, including the home you live in and your shares in the *Vega Corporation*—it could have huge consequences on the company. He could easily mount a takeover—"

"But he's not in my father's will."

"Let me check into the legalities, but I'm not sure it matters. The adoption papers prove your father knew about

Lucas. That gives Lucas rights. I'll get to the bottom of this, and we will deal with it when we have hard facts to work with."

I cast my mind back in time, hoping to dig up anything which might confirm my father had known Brett's mother intimately. But it supposedly happened a decade before I was even born. Then she left Brett and his father when Brett was a baby. Did her decision have something to do with Lucas?

SHAE

I spend the morning tinkering on Ryan's boat, *Gambit*. More and more boats dock in Plymouth. Today's the deadline for all entering boats to berth. At thirty-two feet, *Gambit* is one of the smaller boats in the race, but she's got a new suite of sails. When I took her out yesterday, she was as fast as a racehorse.

Despite England's reputation for gray days and drizzle, today the sky is a deep blue, flecked with wisps of clouds. The breeze is warm, with temperatures in the high sixties, making it possible for me to stick to my usual jean shorts and white tank top ensemble. The sound of raucous laughter floats across from the yacht club as more sailors gather to celebrate and await the start of the race in four days. It's to be a busy time filled with safety checks, briefings, and receptions.

Having skipped breakfast, I walk to the club for one of their famous prawn baguettes. The prawns are tiny, as if someone zapped them with a miniaturizing gun, but the baguette is delicious. I settle at a table near the stretch of windows, taking in the views toward the Mount Batten Peninsula and across Plymouth Sound to Drake's Island. I eavesdrop on people reminiscing around the last Ostar race, how someone once hit a shark, how someone else is doing it to raise money for charity, how this is a great spot to watch the yachts during the America's Cup. Everyone's a lot older than me—and mostly male. I'd read the skipper biographies and I'm the youngest by seven years, and one of two female competitors. I have to find Cassidy, the only other female.

I pan over the bar and lounge area, wondering if I can recognize her from her photo. My pulse spikes and races when I find myself looking into the eyes of someone else who's at a high bar table and already staring at me—Drew Vega.

Our eyes hack into each other's. I clutch the table, even though I'm sitting down. Something twists and shivers in the deepest part of me.

Drew is holding a pint of beer but doesn't attempt to sip or place it on the bar. Next, a little girl of about seven years old, wearing a yellow dress and white cardigan, bowls into Drew. His body reacts to her and he lifts her onto his knee, but his gaze remains on me. Then he swings his attention toward the child as an older, wiry man wearing glasses and a collared T-shirt joins them. They greet each other and Drew scours the bar area to attract the attention of a barman. He flicks his attention to me again. I'm in the exact same position.

I stand sharply and the stool topples. My pulse thumps and crashes, and I bend to pick up the stool and dash out of a side entrance, not daring to glance behind me. *What the hell is he doing here?*

He'd better stay clear of me.

I run, blinking away tears, to hide on *Gambit*. He came to find me in Samoa, risking everything—including my brother's life—then dumped me because I wouldn't instantly say yes to his proposal. *He can't be trusted.*

When I reach *Gambit*, an official requests a random safety

inspection. I step aboard with him and hide below deck. I use my phone to summon an Uber in thirty minute's time. The best thing I can do is hide in my hotel room for the night. It means missing the first of the receptions for the competitors, but I don't care.

Despite my plan, while I'm waiting in the parking lot for a ridiculously late taxi, Drew walks down the stairs from the bar. He's holding the same little girl's hand, the older man following behind. When they reach the grass, Drew swings her onto his shoulders. She squeals and wriggles as he walks, and I realize they're going to walk past me.

I could hide behind a car, run to the other end of the parking lot, but I can't move. Drew spots me and halts. When his friend catches up, Drew says something to him and lifts the protesting child to the ground. She clutches his arms, jumping and objecting, but stops when the man reprimands her.

He's coming over, and you're standing here, frozen. I steel myself and decide to walk to the other side of the lot.

"Shae!"

I quicken my pace. My pulse pelts around my body like a greyhound on a racetrack.

He grabs my elbow. "Surely, we can talk to each other?"

"What's the point?" I spin toward him, surprised at how sharp my words sound.

"The point is we were once... close. We can at least be civil to each other when we bump into each other, can't we?" His eyes flash and I wither inside.

"Why are you here anyway?"

"For the Ostar. My friend Christian is racing. I'm here with him and his family. I assume you're racing?"

"Yes." I fold my arms across my stomach and clutch each elbow, searching for my taxi.

"How's Brett?" he asks, his tone thorny.

"Good. He's studying law at UCLA. Football's become a big part of his life."

I can't look at Drew and keep hunting for the taxi. But the silence becomes stretched, making me peek back at him. His gaze is lost in the horizon and he's doing that thing where his jaw grinds from side to side.

It's as if he remembers I'm there, his head jerks toward me. "Are you going to the reception tonight?" When I say no, he adds, "Not to avoid me, I hope?" He cracks a smile and when it reaches his steel blue eyes, my heart unfolds and flutters in my chest.

I want to scream and pummel myself for continuing to feel so much for him. I want him to hold me and kiss me and love me again, but that can never happen.

"I'm meeting Sienna tomorrow for breakfast," he adds. "She's working in Exeter. I guess Finn told you?"

"No, I... um, heard she and Finn went their separate ways, but I didn't know what she was doing." I'm behaving like a stammering fool and quickly redden. Thankfully, the taxi turns up. "Gotta go," I say.

Drew's face lurches, rapidly stripped bare.

"If you can meet up with me and Sienna, we'll be at the Tea Leaf Café, eight-thirty tomorrow."

I don't look back, don't reply, just open the door to the taxi and throw myself inside.

DREW

I can see the softness underneath Shae's rock-like exterior —it's in the way her eyes flicker with memories and in the way the breath catches in her throat. I'm surprised I can still make her stop breathing just by being near her. It confuses me because she's with Brett now.

The evening reception is an informal supper at the club. I excuse myself, telling Christian I'm jet-lagged. Instead, I mope through the city of Plymouth on foot, half of me needing to clear my head, the other half hoping to bump into Shae. Although I've tried to push her into my past, to cherish the memories but to look forward to a new future, my feelings for her have rushed at me like a breaking wave, swamping me with longing.

I lay awake most of the night, wondering if she'll come to breakfast and remembering what it's like to kiss her, how her body felt beneath me. But imagining her and Brett together leaves me wounded and weak.

The next morning, Sienna is spritely and cheerful, explaining how she transferred her degree from Portsmouth to Exeter because an old boyfriend got a job overseeing the training of guide dogs for the Blind Association.

"His name's Blue," Sienna says, "and we were childhood friends when I lived in Cape Cod. We've been on and off for a while, but he moved to England and we're back on."

I listen as best I can, but my eyes dart to the door every time someone enters the café. It doesn't help that there's a bell on the door, demanding my attention each time it opens.

"You're not your usual self." Sienna's petite face is patched with concern. "You okay?"

"Jet-lagged. Feels like I'm sleepwalking."

"More coffee required. My tip is to go to bed at UK bedtime. You'll adjust faster." I stir my drink and she passes me a second sachet of sugar. "And more sugar. Do you keep in touch with Finn?"

"Not for a while," I say.

"I guess I should ask about Shae. It remains a big mystery —why you disappeared after returning to Samoa."

"She'd moved on." I keep stirring the coffee.

"Ouch. You risked everything to find her and she'd moved on?"

"There was more to it than that."

"You've never enjoyed discussing your love life, have you?"

"Does any man? And no, I haven't spoken to Finn. Not sure why, but he never returns my calls, even after all we went through with Eddie. Shae might've asked him to cut ties."

"He can be a bit of an 'out of sight, out of mind' sort of guy."

I'm done being stuck in the past and finish breakfast quickly, aware I'm terrible company. I consider booking an earlier flight home. I can't bear feeling this way, and the more I think about bumping into Shae again, the more I don't want to. When I first spotted her eating lunch yesterday, my heart felt as if it had been wrenched from my chest and was hanging there, suspended in mid-air, being pulverized like a punching bag. How is it she can have that effect on me after six months of living apart? I thought I'd accepted the fact that she had started a new life but evidently, I haven't.

When I return to my hotel, I book a lunchtime flight to Sydney, which departs tomorrow. Although Christian has no objections to my leaving early as he has his wife here to support him, he won't hear of me bailing out on a second event. He insists I come to the competitor's welcoming reception.

"Besides, half the reason you came out here was to meet people who may help with the America's Cup challenge," he argues.

It's to be a formal dinner and I struggle with my tie. I can't believe I'm nervous, but I tell myself Shae will almost certainly not turn up. From the way she hot-footed it out of the pub yesterday, she's avoiding me as much as I want to avoid her. Besides, she hates crowded parties and wearing dresses.

The yacht club is adorned with fairy lights and the restaurant has morphed into something out of a wedding magazine. White cloths, orange and blue flower centerpieces, and crystal glasses adorn each table and a live band makes it hard to talk. The room is packed. If Shae does come, it'll be easy to avoid each other.

I accept a beer from Christian, gulp it down, and order another. Christian introduces me to several renowned characters in the sailing world, including a crew member from the last America's Cup. I'm unsettled and edgy, slugging drinks and repeating to myself how this time tomorrow I'll be on a plane to Australia where I'll get myself back to normal.

The seating plan is pre-set so when the bell rings, we traipse from the bar into the restaurant, and I follow Christian and Leah, his wife. When we're seated, I nervously check the room and wham—she's there, about to sit at a nearby table. Shae's stunning in an emerald-green strapless dress, which accentuates her tanned skin and dark, treacle-colored hair. She sits two tables over and is spinning her spoon, then her fork. I appreciate how her bare shoulders shift each time she moves, unable to forget how they felt under my hands, under my lips.

She glances my way. I observe her registering me, then her gaze drops. I reach for a wine bottle and top up everyone's glasses.

I spend the evening stopping myself from glancing at her. But every part of me senses her movements and reaches for her.

She doesn't want you anymore.

But I can't live without her. I need to talk to her, maybe even fight for her? When I regard her again, she's talking to the man beside her. I get the urge to leap over the tables and cut in. But then why aren't I doing that to Brett? This is all wrong. She's meant to be with me. I can still make her stop breathing simply by standing near her. She hasn't forgotten what we had. Ava and my inheritance got in the way, that's all. Brett didn't give up on her. Why am I? But can I forgive her for moving on to Brett so quickly? If I could understand what happened... discuss it with her. At the time, she had assumed I'd cheated on her.

The dessert plates are cleared, and coffee is being circulated. People get up and mingle. As soon as the guy next to Shae gets up, I excuse myself to go over to her. But before I reach her, she's on her feet, weaving through the crowd toward the lady's restroom. She looks amazing, her dark hair sleek against the green dress. I start to follow but change my mind, not wanting to act creepy, and go to the bar instead.

There's a queue for the women's restroom. Each time the toilet door opens, I can see the line. When she eventually re-emerges, she seems sleepy and unsteady. Her palm traces along the wall and she starts toward the exit, feeling her way out. *Is she drunk?* She's not a drinker, but maybe, like me, alcohol helped her survive the evening.

She walks into the foyer and bends to slip off her heels. The guy who she was talking to over dinner trails behind. His shoulders are hunched, hands stuffed in his pockets, and he casts around him before shutting the bar door as if checking that no one's seen him leave. *Something's not right.* I leave my drink and follow. Shae isn't in the foyer anymore, but the man drops casually down the stairs and into the night. I loosen my tie and track after him. When I get outside, Shae's resting on a bench and he's standing next to her, his hand on her bare shoulder. He's bent low, talking into her ear.

"Hey, Shae, are you leaving us already?" I saunter toward them to figure out what's going on. The man abruptly straightens and shoves his hands into his pockets.

"Your friend's unwell," he says. "I'll leave you to take over then." He strides off and climbs into a white Mazda parked near the club.

I sit next to Shae, but she sidles sideways. Her strappy silver sandals rest on the bench between us.

"Are you drunk?"

She shakes her head in a way that makes her entire body shudder. "Only had two."

"Are you sick?" But before she can answer she topples forward.

She's out cold.

I dial emergency and crouch on the sidewalk to rouse her. When there's no response, I lay my jacket over her and rest her head on my knees. I've never seen her this vulnerable and my body jumps to protect her. I realize I've managed to keep going all these months only because I knew she was okay and because there was a seed of hope that one day we might work things out. But now, not understanding what's wrong, knowing it's possible to *truly* lose her forever... panic stirs in my gut and I kiss her forehead. *I want you back.*

A sheen of sweat covers her face but her chest rises and falls normally. My breathing becomes erratic as I wait, cursing the slow response of the ambulance. When they do arrive, two paramedics jump into action. They take her vital signs then lift her onto a stretcher.

"Too much to drink?" one asks me.

"No. She had two drinks."

"Sure, she did," he says.

"She had two drinks," I repeat. "I *am* sure. There's something else wrong."

"Any drugs?"

"No. It's something else."

"You coming?" he asks and I jump in with him.

The sirens blare and we jolt back and forth in the ambulance. The monitor shows her heart rate spiking and falling in rotation. They put an oxygen mask on her, and I can't look at her helpless shape without crumbling inside. I study the sea eagle tattoo on her ankle instead.

Moments before we reach the hospital, Shae pulls her knees up to her stomach and screams. They position her on her side and hold her in place, her legs hiked up to her chest. Her eyes are closed as if she's moving through a nightmare. She moans and cries like there's an alien trying to tear open her stomach. Could she be pregnant and losing the baby?

Brett's baby?

SHAE

I'm aware of the beeping of a monitor nearby. Then the bright light behind my eyelids. *I'm in a hospital.* I take a mental scan of my body. There's no pain, merely a stretched sensation in my stomach, and I'm lying on my side. Then I feel the warmth of a hand holding mine. I open my eyes and shut them against the blinding light. But I'd seen someone there. This time I squint first, gradually prising my lids apart.

"Drew." The word is a scratchy whisper. I struggle to swallow. My tongue is stuck to the roof of my mouth. His hair tickles my wrist. When I turn to him, his forehead is on our joined hands. "What happened?"

He lifts his head. "They believe your drink was spiked and you had an allergic reaction, which made the symptoms worse."

A blur of white comes into focus as a nurse looms nearer. "We're awake, are we? How do you feel, Shae?"

"Groggy. Thirsty."

"We've got you on a drip. You simply have a dry mouth. I'll fetch you some water to swill but you mustn't swallow it yet in case it comes up again."

I close my eyes and fall into sleep.

When I next wake, I remember where I am more quickly. Drew's asleep in the chair, his head lolling awkwardly. I want to run my fingers through his hair. Emotion swills around my chest and I gulp back tears. The jerky motion wakes Drew and his face bobs up. He slowly unwraps a smile. *Why had he hurt me so much?*

He pushes the hair behind my ears. A lone tear skids across my cheek into the pillow. I turn away from Drew. He isn't put off and walks to the other side of the bed to see my face. His bare feet are incongruous with the dark charcoal suit trousers. "Still prefer no shoes," I say, more to myself.

He squats, his face in my eyeline. "Old habits..." He shifts my hair out of my eyes, and it feels so right. "But I'm getting help with my apple-sniffing addiction—went to rehab and everything. Some solitary confinement. Took a few months." The backs of his fingers touch my cheek. "I might be re-admitted for a relapse, though." His voice is suddenly intimate.

Is he flirting?

"You shouldn't be here," I say. "You should go."

"Can't, I'm afraid. You have to be released into someone else's care for the next twenty-four hours."

"What day is it?" I push up to sit.

"It's only been overnight, but you've missed the final briefing for the competitors. Christian says he can fill you in, though. It'll be fine. You've got two days to get fit. Doctor says you should be right as rain by tomorrow."

I lay down stiffly, slowly taking in the information. *I won't go soft now.* "I'd rather not be released at all than go anywhere with you."

"That's charming given I've missed my flight to Australia and spent all night watching out for you." His words are filled with humor instead of annoyance. "I kept the police away. My hunch is it was the guy you were next to at dinner. I gave them a full description."

I shiver, realizing I could've been sexually assaulted if it weren't for Drew.

"Thanks. I'm grateful," I say.

He smiles down at me, his concerned eyes tugging at mine.

"But you've hurt me more than any other person ever could, and I can't be around you."

His face becomes stern and rigid. "You don't think you hurt me just as much?"

He *cannot* be equating how I didn't immediately jump at his proposal with how he deserted me!

Drew's raised voice attracts the attention of a passing nurse.

"Okey dokey," she says. "Sir, can you please leave the room for a moment, I need to check over our patient." I observe his mounting frustration climb down and he spins and stalks out. As the nurse checks my pulse and blood pressure, my gaze drops to the floor where my silver sandals from Target are lined up next to Drew's black Armani shoes.

"Is everything okay?" the nurse asks. She eyes the door Drew exited through.

"Can you take his shoes to him and ask him to go?"

THE RACE OFFICIALS are happy to give me a personal briefing after I supply a medical certificate to declare I'm fit to sail. They're shocked at the police visit on my behalf, but no one can identify the man who came to dine next to me. Harry Mathers was the name tag on the table, but the real Harry had pulled out last minute.

It's a rushed final day before the race, and there's no time to wonder why my eyes ache and my vision appears blurry. The doctor hadn't mentioned these potential side effects. I pop some pain killers and continue with my prep.

Journalists interview the competitors and I'm a popular topic, being the youngest girl to compete. I accept all offers, certain the more publicity I receive, the more it'll help me raise funds for my world campaign.

On race day morning, the weather is perfect with a ten-knot wind. I'm excited to get away at midday and leave behind the drama of the last few days. But barely fifteen minutes from leaving my berth, something casts a shadow over the documents I'm reading, and Drew is there. His gaze frisks over me, and he's handsome in blue jeans and white T-shirt.

"Permission to come aboard," he says, grave.

"I'm pretty busy, Drew. The race starts in—"

"It won't take long." He steps across from the jetty and he's suddenly beside me on a boat far smaller than *Sassy*. Quite frankly, the *Titanic* would be too small to hold the both of us right now.

I try to calm my bumping heart and to ignore his lime scent. He reaches forward to touch my hair, but I jerk my head away.

"What are you doing?" I push all my anger into my eyes to ensure there's no room for tears.

A cloud of anxiety hovers on his face. "Isn't there a way of going back in time, Shae?"

"I don't see how." I make my words hard, like throwing stones at him, and then morph myself into rock, unemotional and tough. It usually ensures guys retreat. But he doesn't leave. He looks as if he wants to kiss me, and I half imagine how that would feel, his tongue meeting mine as I wilt against him. Heat pools in my belly and waterfalls toward my groin.

His expression becomes stormy as if a squall went through him. "I still love you, Shae."

I swallow, my heart luffing. "But I can't love you back."

"Because you love Brett?"

"What? Please get off my boat." My brain is stuffed with razor blades and my eyes hurt again. He's always accusing me of being into Brett. Even when we first met.

"Why do I have to take all the blame? Why can't you forgive me if I can forgive you?"

"Not now, Drew. Please leave." I untie the ropes tethering *Gambit* and jump below to flick on the engine. "You have to go, or I'll be disqualified for having you onboard."

I take the helm. He doesn't move. My stomach coils when I observe the shimmer of his tears. As he steps onto the jetty, I almost grab his hand, almost attempt to comfort him. *Almost.*

Gambit drifts from her mooring. Drew watches me, arms hanging limply.

"What did you mean when you said I hurt you, too?" I yell, his words from the hospital haunting me.

He glares at me, lets out a laugh of disbelief. "With Brett? You fell for my best friend and you didn't have the guts to tell me on *Karma*."

"Brett and I are *friends*. That's it. You're the one who dumped *me*. You did all the hurting." The wind whips away my words. I'm not even sure he can hear me. I say them again. His mouth moves in a reply, but short of turning the boat around, I can't understand him. Spotted across the harbor, competitors are on their way to the start line. I must ignore what he said and blast the image of him on the jetty from my mind. *I'm about to cross the Atlantic.*

DREW

G*ambit* motors out to sea, carrying Shae away from me yet again. Shaky with emotion, I drop to the deck and squint into the sun as she grows smaller. The growing ball of frustration inside presses against my ribs and when there's nothing to punch, it becomes hot and thrusts through my body.

Brett and Shae are just friends? But Brett said... the malicious words all over my sketches... they moved to California together. Went to Disneyland.

You're the one who dumped me.

Is that what she thinks? But why?

I figured she'd know I left Samoa because Brett told me the truth about their relationship. But there is no Brett and Shae. What did he tell her? Why does she think I left her in Samoa?

When the starter gun goes off, I scan over the white sails which whizz and weave farther out of sight. The smaller they get, the smaller I feel.

I sit frozen on the jetty, a victim of shock. The area clears out as family and friends head for the bar. I grapple with the strands of thoughts speeding through my brain and attempt to unravel them. It's like trying to fly ten kites at once and not tangle them into one big heap before they fall out of the sky.

Is this Brett's grandest manipulation yet? Surely not even Brett would do something this awful to a best mate simply to win the girl. He's competitive, but is he capable of being this cruel? Maybe he'd got to know her—had fallen for her. I'm struck by the memory of bumping into Shae at the pub and how I can still make her stop breathing.

My phone rings, startling me. I almost hit the reject button, except it's from Gavin.

"Gavin. You have news?"

"I do. I'm afraid all the documentation supplied in Lucas Cunningham's claim has been authenticated. We can contest the exhumation of your father's body, but it's a long shot. A paternity test will certainly rule out his lawsuit if it's negative, but if it's positive, it could mean—well, we discussed this before you left. I understand you're quite open to the idea of having a half-brother, but the implications for *Vega Corp.* and the people who work here, and for your own future. I suppose I'm phoning to ask if you want to fight this?"

I jump to my feet and channel my inner warrior, striding up the jetty. First Brett tries to take Shae from me, now his half-brother is after my company and everything I own? What is it about this family? I also remember the vow I made to the universe that I'd take over the business if we made it back to Samoa safely. "Yes," I say into the phone. "Fight it."

The idea of waiting for a taxi is impossible. Instead, I run back to my hotel. There, I search for Brett's number in my cell. I refuse to wait a month to confirm Shae's words. And I need to find out what he told her and why Shae thinks I left her in Samoa.

Brett.

I met Shae in Plymouth. She told me everything.

Next, I book a flight to Los Angeles.

SHAE

The race winner will complete the crossing in approximately eighteen days. I'll be happy with between three and four weeks. I can do it if I sail through the night—I'm used to the lack of sleep. Finn reckons I stand a chance of winning because when I sailed *Sassy*, I reached Hawaii—a similar distance—in twenty-one days. Some take two months to reach Rhode Island, but I need to impress potential sponsors.

There's something beautiful about the line-up of yachts before a contest—the sound of the luffing canvas, the grins of each skipper, the shapes of the sails against the ultra-blue sky, like a hundred swans in formation. My first solo race. It feels right that I'm here, though Drew's words haunt me.

He's always acted jealous when I mentioned Brett. When I first met Drew in Samoa, I asked about Brett simply to make conversation. It's true I brought him up too much, but then Brett attacked me. How can Drew believe anything could happen between me and Brett after that? Maybe when he discovered we spent weeks together in Samoa, he became bitter and covetous and decided something must've developed between us. How many times do I need to tell him I have no interest in Brett? And if Drew dumped me on a mere *hunch*… well, that's callous. Why didn't he simply ask me?

The megaphone blasts instructions. "Fifty seconds to start." Everyone jumps around their boats, jostling to stay in the best position. They count down from ten seconds.

Within a minute of the starter gun firing, a Corby yacht called *Tatum II* diverts directly into my path and we both jump to keep clear of each other as we make for the breakwater.

The skipper, Colin, I believe, raises his hand and shouts, "Sorry, Shae." I wave off his apology. There's a great atmosphere out here—everyone's cool and not overly dog-eat-dog. I should study the race information and memorize who's on which boat.

During the first few hours, I settle into a position somewhere in the middle of the pack. We whoop and share shouted conversation, exhilaration causing our spirits to soar. With an eighteen-knot wind, the competitors are flying along steadily. As the day dies, we separate though, many of the yachts choosing different routes, some more northerly, some southerly. By tomorrow morning, I'll be on my own, without another boat in sight.

I sail aggressively until sundown, my eyes giving me trouble again. They hurt when I move them, and my vision isn't as sharp. The hospital hadn't mentioned I'd have this problem, but I have to believe it'll pass. It's tiring me out more than normal though, and I set up the autopilot so I can cook dinner.

It's the first time I let myself think about Drew again. I recall his pulled apart expression, his final words. "You fell for my best friend…" I guess it didn't look great when Brett relocated to LA, but I couldn't stop him, and how does that mean I *fell* for him? I'm too exhausted to make any sense of what Drew said, and I head for my bunk, setting the alarm for every thirty minutes to perform checks.

We progress steadily through the thick gloss of night. The stars are tiny chips of light and *Gambit's* sails are ghost-like against the dark backdrop. I listen to the familiar sounds and feel more myself.

When I wake in the silvery dawn glow, the choppy sea resembles scrunched up glittering tin foil reflecting the sun. There's a problem with a line on the boom and I must climb out onto the end of it to replace a rope. It's exhausting as I cling on. I'm not as fit as I was when I made the last crossing, and I'm already craving a hot shower and a freshly cooked meal. *I'm going soft.* The cold dampens my spirits and seeing Drew again has its own weakening effect. I continue to crave him and want to be with him. *I hadn't moved on at all.* But I can't let myself wane. Even if he does still love me, even if he realized leaving me in Samoa was the worst mistake of his life, I can never trust him with my heart again. It doesn't matter how I feel or how he feels. Love is not for me. Look what happened with me and Connor—and my mom and dad.

Next, because there is always something to fix on boats, the leech is fluttering too much. It could shred the mainsail. I head to the front of the main to tighten the leech line. Each time I solve a problem, I become stronger, back in my element. Back where I belong.

The rest of the day is unspoiled as *Gambit* and I skim across the Atlantic. Having an autopilot is a luxury I never had before. It means I can keep racing while preparing food or completing small repairs without having to set up a mechanical wind vane. Competing in a boat I'm unfamiliar with is risky, though. I don't recognize her various noises yet and can't always discern what she's trying to tell me. Consequently, I keep repeating checks to ensure everything's as it should be until we learn to communicate.

On the second day, Mom and Brody call me on the sat phone—another luxury I've never had. They're buoyant with excitement, alongside an undercurrent of worry. Brody informs me of a weather warning. He's tracking both me and the weather radar. Later, Ryan calls to chat and to answer any questions I have about the boat. His voice is full of longing, revealing his wishes that he was here instead of me.

"Before you go," he says. "Brett's been waiting here since yesterday to talk."

Annoyance ripples through me. Brett must've got Ryan's details from Emily. He always goes too far. When I return to LA, we will have a serious discussion. He needs to back off.

"Sorry, Ryan. I hope he's not annoying you. But I have to go now. Tell Brett I'll see him when I finish the race."

In the background, I overhear the grumbling sound of Brett's angry response.

DREW

The next morning, I drive to Heathrow airport, music blasting. I sing and thump my fingers against the steering wheel to distract myself from the roiling anger inside me. The flight is non-stop, and I spend the entire twelve hours staring out of the window at the blue sky and stiff clouds or at the ocean below. Knowing Shae is below me, crossing the Atlantic, dislocates my brain—is it possible she could look up and see me flying overhead?

I'm going to sort this out once and for all. I'll confront Brett and insist on the truth. If he's done what I think he has... I swallow hard and push back at the rising fury. The knowledge he's lied to me, that he's caused this rift between me and Shae, has ignited a seething ball of fire inside me. If only I'd gone to the hotel in Samoa with Shae instead of visiting Brett on *Sassy*, but I was putting off a confrontation with her family. I admit that now. Finn had confirmed Kathleen was seriously angry that I'd dragged him, and then Shae, into the situation with Eddie. Avoiding confrontations has always made everything worse—look where it got me with my father. We had no relationship for years because I avoided tackling the issues between us—I even escaped to Samoa to evade him.

I have no idea where Brett lives in LA—or Shae. I drive to the UCLA campus and I'm forced to wait on a wall by a fountain in hope of spotting him. But there's no sign of him and I have to give up and book a room at the Beverly Hills Hilton. It conjures memories of how I flew into LA to surprise Shae after she was acquitted of the charges connected to Connor Stratton. It had been an amazing night and we made love for the first time in a bed, rather than on *Sassy*. But nothing has gone right since. My father died, and Shae took off to Samoa on *Ariel,* then ran off to LA with Brett.

The next day I wander the campus again. It's huge though, and Brett could be anywhere. I target the faculty of law and sit on the stairs at the entrance to the red brick building. I consider finding an admin office to ask where he lives but I'm guessing they won't give out private information to a complete stranger.

While I wait, I remember how Shae had once expressed her confusion, wondering why I hadn't confronted Brett after he attacked her on the beach. I wasn't able to properly explain it to her then, except that I felt sorry for him after what he went through with the kidnapping and his father not paying the ransom. I'd made allowances for him for years because of it—letting him do as he pleased, covering for his drinking and drugs, permitting him to muscle in on the girls I was keen on, even taking the rap for his shoplifting once. The confrontation about to take place should've happened years ago. Finally, I'm ready for it.

The whole time I'm waiting, Lucas Cunningham sits in the rear of my mind like a toad in a dark room. Should I tell Brett he has a half-brother? If Lucas does receive half of my inheritance, where does that leave Brett? Nowhere, I guess, unless he joins forces with Lucas—who knows what they'd do. Take over the company? Brett was willing to turn Shae over to the police to collect the reward... he would do anything to ensure he is no longer dependent on his father for financial security.

I march across the campus again, determined to stay as long as it takes to find Brett. The grounds are spotted with seemingly ancient trees and the neatly clipped lawns invite you to rest. Mature green vines grow up the sides of buildings and groups of students criss-cross en route to somewhere. I'm about to start climbing a three-flight set of stairs in the gardens when I spot him. He's near the top, lightly descending each step as he's done every day for months.

The rage pulsing through me is ferocious, and I'm glad he's at the top. I take in deep breaths to calm myself. My body crackles, a lit firecracker. When he drops down the last few stairs, I finally blow and pile into him, scrunching his shirt in my fist, shoving until he trips backward onto the steps. He grunts in surprise, his hands moving to stop his fall as I punch him and pull myself upright. He rolls onto his front, holding his jaw and daring to peer at me from his position sprawled on the ground.

"Drew. Friggin' hell, take it easy." His words infuriate me further and I close in on him. He jumps up, a few steps higher than me, palms outstretched. "Calm down. We can talk."

"What's there to talk about? You lied. You didn't think about her when you lied. You hurt her. How could you do that to her... to me?" Spit flies from my mouth and rage builds and builds.

He hovers above me and wipes his hand across his bloody nose. "I fell in love with her, mate. What can I say? And I *did* believe you guys were over. By the time I found out you were coming for her it was too late."

"No way, Brett. That's not good enough. She told me you were friends and there is no relationship. You told me a very

77

different story. You said you'd slept together and that she told you she loved you. You sent me emails leading me to believe you were living together."

His face contorts. "Did she say we were just friends?"

"You got rid of me and hoped she'd turn to you instead? If you really loved her, you wouldn't have done something so awful to her. What did you tell her? She must have wanted to know why I left her in Samoa?"

Brett unexpectedly sits on a step, hanging his head.

"What did you tell her?"

"Does it matter? Nothing ever happened between us, not even a kiss."

"Then was it you who wrote all over my sketches and stabbed them with a pencil?"

"That actually *was* Shae."

"Oh." My heart sinks like when *Sassy* dropped down the front of a huge wave. "I don't understand. She thought those things she wrote?"

"She wrecked the sketches the day she saw you with Ava. The day she sailed out of Sydney Harbor. That's the truth."

His words are a salve to my anger. "Jeez, Brett. I've been trying to make sense of this for months. None of it hung together and you're the reason. You and your lies." I slump, exhausted. I had barely slept during the last few days. "Just tell me… put me out of my misery. Why does she think I left her in Samoa?"

We've attracted a crowd and they observe us from a few meters away. Brett pastes on a grin and waves.

"Everything okay, Brett?" a guy in a UCLA tracksuit top asks.

Brett stands slowly as if his legs might give way. "Yeah, it's cool, Neil. Thanks." He steps down the stairs and walks past me. "Come on. Unless you want an audience."

I follow, again pushing back the ferocious heat inside me. We stride side by side, saying nothing. When we reach a deserted café, Brett sinks into a chair at one of the outside tables. I sit opposite him as he rubs at his eyebrows roughly, then wipes a palm over his cheek, now pink and slightly swollen.

"I'm sorry," he says. He flexes his jaw, checking it works. "It was a spur of the moment thing. I didn't plan it—the lies. When you told me she hadn't agreed to marry you, it seemed like my last chance to have her. Or I convinced myself I had a chance. I love her, Drew." He lifts his gaze to me. The painful truth is right there. "I couldn't imagine life without her. So, I lied to you and I told her..."

He grips the arms of the chair, his wounded eyes sweeping the area behind me.

"What did you tell her?"

"That you were angry she hadn't said yes to your proposal straight away."

My body lurches upright and I lunge across the table at him. He stands so I can't reach him. I stride around the table, throwing his chair aside. We square up.

"What's your problem?" he yells. "You've won, haven't you?"

"This isn't some competition, Brett. It's my life. It's Shae's life and you've..."

The surge of fury that engulfs me could lead to trouble, to being arrested. He's confirmed what I needed to know. I want to hurt him like he's hurt me, but it's not going to change anything, and no amount of fighting will hurt him enough.

When I walk away, I hear his following footsteps, but I step up my pace.

"Drew. Wait. I'm sorry, yeah. Love makes us do crazy things, doesn't it?"

I swing around to face him. He halts, keeping his distance. I stab my finger at him. "Never come near me again. Never call, never email." His expression spins from defensive to surprised.

"Come on, Drew. We can move past this. Twenty years of friendship."

This time I can't help myself and I'm in his face, fisting his shirt. "We will *never* get past this." I shove him.

Shae thinks I dumped her because she didn't accept my proposal!

"And I'm going to tell Shae the truth. She's never going to want to see you again."

I ignore Brett's final parting shot. "I wouldn't be so sure of that, mate."

At my hotel, I read a text message from my PA asking if I'll be returning to the office soon. Instead of replying, I book a flight to Newport, Rhode Island.

SHAE

Today the sky is peppered with black puffs of cloud. Behind them, the sun trims their edges in effervescent light. It feels unreal, like sailing inside a painting. It's my fifth day, and the Atlantic and I remain friends. She was mutinous overnight, but the clouds have nurtured her into liquid mercury. My only real concern is the pain in the back of my eyes, especially bad when I'm puffed out. Sometimes my vision seems off and the bright blue of the scenery becomes covered in a film of gray. I'm also getting headaches. I suppose the drug that spiked my drink is still having an effect.

Half a dozen pods of dolphins have just finished entertaining me and gone to find someone else to play with. I settle onto some cushions and bathe in the peace. Occasionally, the ocean fills with crystallized light. It's as if the sun has swooped down and is swimming in it. My hair streams behind me, my scrunchie lost once again. I spend these times planning my solo campaign. I make list after list, and I imagine what it'll be like to be alone, without human contact for nine months or more. It doesn't scare me one bit. I crave the solitude and the haven of the ocean. I especially love twilight when the world turns golden just moments before the sun winks goodbye, and I'm in a people-less place beyond the sunset.

That afternoon, I'm running through some checks and small repairs when I notice the main's halyard sheave is stiff. With a minimum of sixteen days of racing left, I mustn't ignore it. I decide to go up the mast to lubricate it. The day is fairly calm with a twelve-knot wind and clear skies.

I unpack the bosun's chair. It's apparently safer than using harnesses as I sit in the seat, strapped in for safety, similar to a toddler's swing. Then I use a pulley system to lever myself up and down the mast.

When I near the top of the mast, I let myself hang there to rest my straining arms and gape out to sea. It's spectacular. The mushrooming ocean curves, making it seem like I'm on the edge of the world.

I lubricate the sheave and check on the halyards, spreaders, and pins, and then it's as if *Gambit* sails into a brick wall. I hear a thud and the bosun chair jerks and swings wide, completely out of control. I spin in the air like a diving, whirling kite. When I look below, the shadow of a whale drifts past us. *Had we hit it?* Momentum flies me toward the mast, and I reach to brace for a hit but my bony spine slams into it. My skull strikes it with such force a murky ink spreads through my brain until everything is dark and slow and quiet.

Consciousness creeps up on me alongside nausea and a splitting headache. I'm hanging over the edge of the bosun's chair, swinging around the mast. I straighten, but it's like swaying with a bag over my head because I can't see a thing. I widen my eyes but there's nothing to see. Fear pecks at me. I must've been hanging here for hours; there are no stars or moon tonight. My pulse shatters through me as I search for the end of the rope to lower myself. It's so dark I can't even make out my hands in front of my face. It's as if we're gliding inside a bowl of blackness. Something's not right. I've sailed into a blackhole.

When my feet hit the deck, I unstrap myself and crawl to the companionway, my head thumping with pain. Below deck, seawater sloshes above my ankles. I search for a Coleman lantern to determine why that might be and realize none of the instrument lights are lit. Groping for the switch, I flick on the running lights, but nothing happens. My feet splash through what's like a pond and I remember the whale. *We're taking on water.* I resume my search for a lantern, but the gloom is too thick, and the collision will have knocked it out of place.

If I could see, I wouldn't have panicked, but when it takes an age to find a bucket, fear becomes heavy inside me. I can barely breathe. I bail water but I can't check how effective I'm being. I have to admit defeat. I grasp for the emergency beacon which will alert authorities as to my position. It's securely in its bracket and I remove it and press the button.

This is it. My race is over. We're sinking.

There are no lights on the beacon though. It makes no sense as even if the entering water has affected the electrics, the beacon is battery-operated. I search for the inflatable dinghy, harness it, and send it overboard, ready to jump into if I have to. Then I go below with the bucket. Nausea overwhelms me and sleepiness gnaws at my bones. I fight it, recognizing I probably have a concussion. The next time I chuck a bucket of water into the ocean, I throw myself forward and vomit into the sea. I stop and wait for the wave of queasiness to lessen.

"Come on," I say and stand, tottering and dizzy. My brain is fuzzy, making it hard to think.

I keep bailing water, but I'm too slow and the level doesn't reduce. *I must. I must.* Unused to having communications onboard, I remember my sat phone. But will it work? Despite the numbers not lighting up, they beep as I press each one to dial Brody. The line crackles. I wriggle my fingers but can see nothing. Then I hear Brody's sweet voice.

"Shae. Are you okay?"

"No. I've hit a whale and I was knocked unconscious when the bosun's chair smashed me into the mast. I don't know where I am or what time of day it is. All the lights are out, and it's pitch dark. No moon. Not a single star. We're taking on water and I don't think the emergency beacon is working."

Brody keeps me talking, disregarding the cost. He's in touch with the rescue authorities who have picked up my signal. A merchant ship has diverted its course to pick me up.

"What if it hits me? None of my lights work and I can't find the lanterns in the pitch black."

"Hang on, Shae." I listen to him type.

"Shae, based on your location, it's nine o' clock in the morning there. How can it be dark?"

A spike of fear ricochets through me. "I sailed into a black hole when I was unconscious. Is there something similar to the Bermuda Triangle out here?"

"No, of course not. When you were knocked out, it might've affected your sight."

Nausea overwhelms me and I vomit onto the deck.

Is it possible for a blind person to solo sail around the world?

DREW

S hae sits propped up in the bed, staring through the wall ahead of her. While I tell her what Brett did, how he manipulated and deceived us both, her demeanor barely changes. In fact, her expression hasn't changed from vacant since they brought her into the hospital a week ago.

Outside, the London traffic hums and it's the only sound in the room. I wish I was a mind reader.

Staring blankly, Shae uncrosses her arms. "I'll deal with Brett."

That's it? What about us? What about our future?

Shae presses the button to lower her bed. "I'm tired. I need some sleep."

I'm aware she has a lot on her plate. She's questioning why her sight hasn't returned, and the doctors aren't sure why either, or even *if* her vision will return, but shouldn't she be turning to me rather than pushing away now she knows the truth?

"I'm here for you, Shae. I never stopped loving you. Please, lean on me. Let me help you through this."

"My mom's here. You should go back to Sydney." She

stares through the ceiling, her arms stiff by her sides. "I'm sure you have work to do, pressing deadlines."

I recall Lucas and how I should be at the office to discuss any new developments. I'd decided not to tell Shae about him. His claim didn't affect her, or us.

"Did you hear anything I've said?" I ask. "I don't want to be apart from you anymore. I want to build a future with you, and now that the truth is out, we can. Can't we?"

"I'm not the same person," she replies. "I'm not Shae the sailor, the adventurer, the Gotta Go Girl. I'm not the person you fell in love with. I'm blind. I'm an invalid. A liability. Why discuss us or the future? I have no future."

"Don't, Shae. This is simply another blip and we'll get through it. I'll find the best medical experts and you'll regain your sight—"

"My eyesight is the one thing your billions cannot buy. No, I'm not risking getting in deep again. I won't be the burden you have to live with. The burden you're guilted into staying with because how could you leave a *blind* girl?"

Finally, her expression changes and her mouth twists. Tears swell and she blinks them away.

I rush to comfort her, but it's like hugging a mast. A moment later, she pulls back.

"You're not helping," she says. "I can't deal with 'us' right now. Please, give me some space. What if I can never sail again? What job can I do if I'm blind? Where will I live? I don't have room for what you make me feel."

Hope blooms. "But I do make you feel?"

She tugs the covers over her body to her neck as if to hide from me. "Do I have to call the nurse to get you to leave?"

SHAE

How many times is the universe going to tell me love is not for me?

Outside the hospital room, a bird cries out as if calling for me. It sounds like a bigger bird. A hawk? I lean forward to sight it before realizing that's not possible. I can no longer admire the circling sea eagles or see the stars or moon to navigate by. When Drew and I are parted again, I won't be able to find Sirius.

The truth about Brett isn't truly a shock. I had seen and ignored the signs of his possessive nature. He had refused to leave me alone or give up on making me love him. I'd trivialized how he had lost his temper or sulked when I didn't respond to his gestures in the right way. At least he wasn't drinking and partying. I shouldn't have kept the incident with the gun in Samoa from Drew, but I hadn't wanted him to fight with Brett. That's where I went wrong. If I'd told Drew, he might've questioned Brett's lies. Why didn't I take Brett's behavior more seriously? I'm always accusing Drew of being too soft on Brett, but *I'm* worse. There's something wounded about Brett though—and both Drew and I wanted to heal him.

Later, I ask to borrow Mom's cell and call Emily.

"You're all over the news again," she says. "You gave me a near-heart attack. But you seem to have nine lives, like a cat."

"Yes, I'm alive," I say, though I feel dead inside. We discuss the race, the accident, and how my drink was spiked. The media doesn't know I've lost my sight yet, and I don't mention it now, either. I'm not ready to deliberate over it or have people sympathize and pity me. I change the subject to Brett, needing to explain how she should avoid being alone with him. "Have you hung out with Brett much lately?"

"I haven't seen him since you left," Emily says. "He only comes around to be with you anyway. He's clearly besotted."

I had intended to tell her how unpredictable he is, how he attacked me, the incident with the gun, how he'd caused the rift between me and Drew, and to warn her off him. But I realize she's completely safe from Brett—it's only me he has eyes for.

"When will you be home?" Emily asks.

Her question throws me, not only because LA doesn't feel like home, but because I can no longer picture how my life in LA will be. How will I take a flight as a blind person? How will I get a job, move from place to place? Can I even go back there? Tears clog my throat. "I'll text you. But I've got to go."

Every dream I had is gone. The happiness I was trying to find through sailing can never be. I have to let it all go. But I won't allow Drew to sacrifice his life and happiness for me. Friendship is all we're destined to have. I'd also promised myself that I'd never get trapped in a relationship like Mom did. Being with Drew as a blind woman would entrap me. I need to do this by myself.

I always believed I was meant to sail this world alone. Except, now I can't even sail.

DREW

Through the window, I track the circling flight of some sort of falcon above the vast grounds of the London hospital. It reminds me of Shae's sea eagle tattoo though its 'hyaik-hyaik' call cuts through the silence like an alarm. I pull in a lungful of air as if I just remembered to breathe.

"I can't bear seeing Shae so defeated," I say. "She's a shell of herself. All her spirit has drained away."

Shae's mother leans over the table and covers my hands with her cool, thin fingers. "Shae's strong. She'll get back on course. It's only been two weeks." From the way her expression buckles, I know she's not convinced. "Cup of tea?" She reaches for the teapot she ordered from the near empty hospital café. She resembles Jamison—a cuppa is always the answer to a crisis.

"An eye specialist is talking to her now," I say. "He's got a flawless reputation and is reviewing her case." *I'm hanging all my hopes on him.*

Kathleen flattens her palms against her chest. "Drew, we can't afford him. Not unless Ryan's insurance covers it."

"I'll cover it. Don't worry."

"I can't let you do that."

"We want the best for Shae, don't we?"

She purses her lips, then sets to pouring milk and tea and stirring. "Why did you leave Shae in Samoa?" she asks. "Shae never talked about it. She said you'd chosen different paths. But you're here now—even before *I* could get here."

I rub the back of my neck. "Long story. Brett manipulated us… he came between us." I pause and add, "He betrayed us both."

"*No!* How awful. Does Shae know?" Kathleen passes me a cup and saucer, her eyes wide with surprise.

"Thanks," I say. "Yes. She does. I told her a few days ago." *Not that the truth changed anything between us.* I take a sip of the scalding tea.

A small man with a neat white beard, wearing a doctor's coat over a pinstripe suit, strides directly toward me and Kathleen.

"You must be Dr. Carlton?" I stand and accept his handshake.

"And you must be Drew Vega and Shae's mom?" Kathleen nods. "We've completed further tests," he adds, "and I have some promising news."

Kathleen clutches my arm.

"Shae told me she had eye pain and blurry vision before the accident. She believed it was the result of her drink being spiked a few days before the race started."

Kathleen sucks in a breath, frowning at me. I doubt Shae told her about the incident.

"Her symptoms previous to the incident on the boat, along with my tests, indicate the vision loss is not due to the accident. Unfortunately, the hospital staff jumped to the wrong conclusion, but my diagnosis is this is a clear case of optic neuritis."

"Which means?" Kathleen says, naked with hope.

"It means her optic nerves are swollen. The causes are somewhat unknown—possibly it's an autoimmune response or possibly it's due to some sort of bacterial infection. We comprehend little about what triggers the condition, but we do know she's liable to regain her sight. The neuritis is often a pre-cursor to multiple sclerosis, but the tests show no markers for the disease, therefore once the inflammation reduces, her vision should return."

"How long will it take?" I ask.

"Anywhere from three weeks to three months, sometimes longer."

"What treatment does she need?"

"The long and short of it is, nothing. Some use intravenous corticosteroids for a while but there's no proof it changes the final outcome and the side effects can include depression, gut problems, and insomnia. I'd say, given the concussion, rest and time is all she needs."

"She'll definitely regain her sight?" I could run to the moon and back.

"In most cases, yes. But there's a small chance her vision won't return, or of reoccurrence." Dr. Carlton shrugs. "It's unusual to occur in both eyes simultaneously, but I see no reason why she won't fully recover." He smiles at Kathleen, then me.

"Thank you, doctor," Kathleen says. She pumps his handshake, then hugs him. He grins in a good-natured way. "Nice to give you better news."

After he leaves, we abandon our tea and return to the ward. We flank Shae's bed. She resembles a corpse—unmoving, expressionless, blankly staring. Kathleen leans in to kiss her cheek and hug her.

"It could be six months, Mom," Shae says, her expression frozen. "Or I might be one of the unlucky ones and never recover. Don't fool yourself."

"But we have hope, Shae."

I long to touch Shae, to reassure her. But it's not the right time. She's still saying we should take it slow. She hates feeling useless—she called herself pointless—and wonders how I can even love her. This has cut her off at the knees and I'm wondering how many more times she can survive being felled.

———

"HELLO, GEORGE. IT'S DREW."

"Hey yup, son. How are you? I was hoping to hear the latest. I saw the news abou' Shae. How is she?"

"A bit of a train wreck but alive at least. She could have drowned out there."

"I heard i' was a close call—boat was going down? Is she there? Can I talk to her?"

"She's not. I'll get her to call you soon, but I wanted to speak to you first. You might be able to help. Shae has an infection of the optic nerves. She's temporarily blind."

George sighs deeply before a flat voice asks, "What do you mean, temporarily?"

"It should return, once the inflammation reduces. It could take weeks but probably three or four months."

"She must be devastated. Someone like Shae... jeez. How will she cope without sailing? It's who she is. She resembles me. It's what grounds us and makes us feel as if we have a place in this world."

I agree with what he's saying, and recall how sailing has helped me, too. For Shae, it's a lifelong thing though; for me, merely months. "That's why I'm calling," I say. "If she can somehow sail while recovering it could make all the difference. I've never seen her this defeated... like a lifeless doll. Do you believe it's possible she can skipper a yacht while blind?"

"Of course. Takes a bit of learnin' but I have a friend who's a sailor and can't see farther than the end of his nose. Where are you calling from?"

"London. But she's agreed to stay in Sydney with me."
Reluctantly.

"You're back together? What happened? She told me you left Samoa without a word. I'm meant to be mad a' you. You hurt my girl."

"Yeah, I'd be mad at me, too, if I were you. It was a misunderstanding. Brett convinced me that he and Shae were into each other, and I should clear out for her sake. He said I was putting her in a terrible situation, making her choose between him and me. He's a bloody credible liar." I recall the sketches he showed me, with her handwriting and how she desecrated them. "Then he followed Shae to LA and made it seem as if they were living together."

The line goes quiet again, and I can hear the soft sound of the ocean crashing onto the beach outside George's cottage.

"I told Shae he was trouble," George says. "Would she listen? Tha' boy's capable of anything to get wha' he wants. Where is he now?"

"Last I heard, he was in LA."

"I haven't said anything before because I didn't realize Brett was in her life. But the reason I wasn't on the beach welcoming you both back after she went out to rescue you was because Brett attacked me. Knocked me out. Cracked my skull and I ended up in hospital."

"*What?*"

"When Shae left on *Ariel*, he lost it, throwing and kicking things in the cottage, ranting. I tried to calm him down, and he picked up a lamp and hit me."

"He's gone too far. Did you report him?"

"He'd flown out of Samoa by the time I reported it. He's not right in the head, that boy. Or it's drugs. Although Shae said he was clean then."

"Sorry, George. Sorry I brought him to your doorstep."

"Never blame yourself for your friend's faults."

"He's no friend of mine anymore."

"I'm glad to hear it. What can I do to help?"

I take a deep breath. "I was hoping you'd get *Sassy Jam* seaworthy again."

George and I talk for an hour. We discuss how to find a mast for *Sassy* because he's pretty much fixed the rest of her over the last seven months. And we figure out how to get her to Sydney. *At least it's not cyclone season.*

"Shae's agreed to come and live with you, then?" George asks.

"Temporarily." I push aside the memory of her unhappy expression when she agreed that returning to LA wasn't possible without any family help. Given she can't work— well, not immediately—how would she pay rent and medical, shop and cook, or go to doctor appointments? *Those were just the main obstacles.* Besides, we had reconciled since Brett's confession, even if we were keeping it friends-only for now.

"And if Brett's there, then it's another reason not to be in LA," George points out.

"Exactly, and Townsville's not ideal. Her mother lives in a small, cramped cottage in the middle of nowhere. There are no buses, her mother doesn't drive, and the pathways are rocky and made of dirt. No sidewalks. It'd be too hard for Shae to gain independence. She'd be a prisoner with her mother as jailor."

I'd told Shae how Jamison could help her, and how Mrs Jones does the cooking and shopping, and Shae could use my chauffeur and fly on the jet to visit her mom when she wants. Adding up everything, she had finally relented. She'd run out of choices.

Next, I call Finn. He drums his fingers on the table by the phone while we're talking, and he's excited by my proposition—to go to Samoa and bring *Sassy Jam* to Sydney with George.

"I figure if Shae is going to sail without her sight," I say, "having *Sassy Jam*, a boat she knows like the back of her hand, will make it a whole lot easier."

"That's really good of you, Drew." He stops drumming and there's silence. "Hey, I'm sorry I kind of lost touch. I had to support my sister, yeah? But my mom explained what Brett did and why you left Samoa."

"I understand. It's what a brother *should* do." I remember how I used to view Brett as a brother, and maybe once he was.

"This is a great idea," Finn says. "Mom says Shae's spirits are low. It's exactly what she needs. My sister needs to sail like the ocean needs salt."

"I reckon she's more depressed about not being able to sail than she is about losing her sight." We chuckle, even though it's probably the truth. I remember how Shae had gone stir crazy after not being out on the water for just two weeks in Townsville. Sailing is the one thing that will lift her enough to re-ignite that strength inside her so she can get through the next few months without her spirits spiralling. "George is working as fast as he can, but I'll stay in touch."

Even if Shae can't let herself love me, I can't avoid loving her. It means I must back off while doing everything I can to guide her through this.

Sassy Jam is the only friend who can truly help her.

SHAE

I live inside a dark cave. And it may as well have bars.

Once I'm released, Drew flies us all to Sydney on his private jet. I listen to Mom's exclamations—the wide leather seats, the trays of cold meats and cheeses, the air hostesses and the smart uniforms they wear. The pilot comes to introduce himself. But I can see none of it. I pretend to sleep for most of the flight, knowing the ocean is below us, knowing I can't sail on it—maybe ever.

When we arrive in Sydney, Mom will go on to Townsville, while I've decided to stay with Drew. The idea of having to live with either of them wasn't appealing, but what choice do I have? After being acquitted of the charges against Connor, a few days living with Mom in Townsville had pulled me down and I had felt low and trapped. She had treated me like a child, monitoring what I ate, when I slept, and how much fresh air I was getting. She also tried to persuade me not to sail anymore because it was too dangerous. In addition, she lives in the most impractical of places for someone who is blind. Then there's her depression, which often means she's admitted to a clinic. In the end, the only viable option was to accept Drew's offer. We're just friends though, and it's temporary.

When Drew goes to visit the pilot, Mom sidles nearer. "Why are you acting cold toward Drew?" she asks. "He's explained what Brett did. He's done nothing wrong. Can you not get past this? He's obviously besotted with you."

"What if I'm blind forever? Everything could change. *I* might change. How can I let myself love him again if I am no longer the person he fell for? It's not right to reclaim our relationship with that possibility on the horizon." I love him and I won't do that to him.

"You have to remain hopeful and optimistic. The doctor is."

"Until I regain my sight, I won't take any chances. I couldn't deal with it if we picked up where we left off, and then he regretted it, but stayed with me out of pity. Worse, what if he moved on with someone else—someone who isn't a burden—and I lost him again? Besides, he deserves to be with a woman he can live a full life with, not an invalid who'll bring him down. How could I ever be a fit mother to his children or a fit wife to accompany him on charity balls?"

"Blind people can live full and normal lives, honey. You're being melodramatic."

I shrug, wanting to add that I'm not exactly feeling lovable or desirable. The idea of making love when blind... I'm vulnerable enough. "Let me make my own choices, Mom. I need to wait until I regain my vision—or not—before I decide on anything. For now, we're friends. Drew understands."

At Sydney airport, Drew helps me disembark. We navigate the steps and climb aboard what seems to be a golf cart. The lime scent of him is reassuring, and I both love and dislike his touch—it reminds me how if he let me go, I'd be lost in a sea of darkness. It reminds me how dependent I am on him. The hospital gave me a white cane, but it makes me feel as if I'm someone else. It labels me as a person who is helpless, broken. I can barely recognize myself.

Drew continues to guide me through the emigration process, and I'm confused and overwhelmed by something I've done a dozen times. Worse, when we emerge into the main airport, every reporter in Sydney is there. The noise scares me. They surround us, as they had when we docked in the Gold Coast on *Sassy*. Unable to see them, I cling to Drew.

"Will you ever sail again, Shae?"

"Are you back together, Mr. Vega?"

Drew increases the pace and I trip over my feet, though he stops me tumbling to my knees. Next Drew's driver, Arnold, says he's pleased to meet me, and he takes my hand to put it into his for a handshake. It's a sweet gesture, but it makes me want to cry. Being driven without seeing where we are is disconcerting. If I felt I didn't fit anywhere before, now I truly know it.

When we pull up to Drew's house, my shoes crunch on the gravel driveway as I climb out of the car. Drew's beside me, his arm around my waist.

"We're going to go up five stairs to the front door," he says cheerfully. I picture the entrance to Drew's home as I remember it from that awful day—the stairs over a bridge to the front door with water features on either side.

"Good morning, Miss Love. Welcome. Please come in." I remember Jamison's proper English accent. I re-imagine his formal expression from before, even though his eyes had sparkled with warmth under unruly eyebrows. He'll be wearing his suit, like it's the 1940s and he's living on an estate in Oxfordshire, England rather than in a harborside mansion in Sydney. This time, I notice he smells of ginger and laundry powder.

"Two more steps, Shae," Drew whispers, and we step upward into a space that's colder than the air outside.

"Thanks for holding the fort, Jamison." Drew's words are laced with fondness.

I remember the mirrored hallway, the black and white-marble floor, the eight-foot-tall tropical trees.

"I can take you to your room, Miss Love, where you can have tea and freshen up, or would you prefer to come down for refreshments?" Jamison's voice is calm, measured, polite.

"In my room, please" I want to crawl into bed and stay there.

"Thank you, Jamison. It was a long flight," Drew explains.

"Allow me to lead the way," Jamison says.

I shuffle next to Drew.

"Lots of stairs next, Shae."

I lift one foot, place it on a carpeted stair, then lift the other, slow like a toddler. By the time we reach the top, I want to throw myself on the ground, pummel the floor, and cry. I hate the new me. Everything is wrong about her, not only on the outside but on the inside, too.

"You'll become more familiar with the house, and once you start using your stick, you'll do this by yourself," Drew says.

"This is Miss Love's suite," Jamison says. I hear a door open.

Drew guides me inside and a breeze brushes across my cheeks and lifts my hair. I notice the sound of the tinkling of rigging. "I asked Jamison to make up this room because it's like standing inside an ocean wave," Drew says. "The walls are aqua blue and everything else is white—the carpet, the bed, the bed covers."

I want to ask, "What's the point of putting me in here when I can't see it?" but he's being thoughtful, and he thinks describing what I can't see helps. Except, the effect has me feeling even more helpless, and I want to tell him to stop sounding so sunny.

"There are two sets of French doors, which open onto a

balcony with a view of the harbor and the yachts," Drew continues. "The sheer curtains are fluttering in the breeze. It's peaceful. You can rest here."

"There's an en-suite bathroom," Jamison adds. "I counted ten steps from the end of the bed to the door of the bathroom, Miss Love. You can check if our strides are similar."

"Thank you," I say quietly.

"I'll set you on the edge of the bed," Drew says, moving me forward again. When my feet kick the bed's base, I sit down and am swallowed by a hefty, voluminous duvet.

"Mr. Vega requested I order some garments for you. I used a personal shopper from David Jones. The clothes are in the wardrobe."

I make myself smile. "That was thoughtful of you both."

"Miss Love, there's a comfortable setting on the balcony. Shall I bring a tray for you to have out there?"

"Thanks, but I want to sleep." To be alone where no one is fussing, explaining the things surrounding me or guiding my every step.

"You shouldn't sleep until nearer night-time, or you'll take longer to get over the jet lag," Drew says.

"Jet lag is the least of my problems." My tone is sharp, and I instantly regret my words. The subsequent silence is more than awkward. I imagine the expressions on their faces. "Sorry, I'm tired… and overwhelmed. I need to be alone for a while. To rest. To find my bearings. Please."

"Of course," Jamison says. "I've placed a bell on this bedside table." There's a sound of a bell tinkling. "Should you need anything at all, please ring it. I've put a glass of water there, too."

I thank him, and following a pause, he treads away from us.

Drew pats my shoulder. "This is new and scary, but you'll become familiar with the house and Jamison's always here to help." When I say nothing, he adds, "I'll let you settle in." He places my white stick in my hand.

After the door clicks shut, I stand and count ten paces, waving the stick ahead of me to avoid crashing into furniture. The carpet changes to tiles, which must indicate the start of the bathroom. But where's the toilet? I grope around, overwhelmed by humiliation, and find the basin, a walk-in shower, towels hung on the wall, then finally, the toilet. I strip off my clothes, craving a shower to wash the long journey from my body. It takes a while to figure out the hot from the cold tap, but the stream of water that rushes over me calms me. And the shampoo smells of apples.

"As subtle as a brick through a window, Drew." My words echo in the bathroom.

Wrapped in a towel and back in the bedroom, I have no idea where the wardrobe is. I'm not up to fumbling around to find handles that may not exist if they're sliding doors. I might bump into tables or chairs, too. Instead, I slide into bed naked.

No need to shut the curtains to darken the room.

The breeze coming through the open French doors cools my face as I snuggle deeper under a cover which is warm yet light as a cloud. I listen to the voices of the tinkling yachts in the harbor below, the sea gulls, the comings and goings around me. I'm dead inside and full of hate for a world that constantly hands out hurt.

I doze in and out of sleep.

At some point, I'm nodding off again when I hear someone move in the room. Not in the mood for a talk, and knowing I'm naked under the covers, I pretend to be asleep. The air coming through the balcony doors is now brittle with cold. It's winter in Sydney, even though it is June. The skin on my face is icy. But I enjoy the tinkling of the boat's rigging outside and the sound of crashing waves.

Whoever is there remains silent. It must be Drew,

checking up on me, deciding on whether to wake me or not to ensure I slip into the right sleep pattern. Listening carefully, I identify the sound of steady breathing. At one point, the breathing becomes heavy and deep. Then there's a stifled groan, and it doesn't sound like Drew at all. I try to catch the lime scent of him, but only the faint smell of sweat reaches me. I wait for him to leave. After what seems a long time, there's the muffled movement of footfalls receding, the thick carpet absorbing his footsteps. I'm too tired to assume anything but that he left the room. Sleep clutches at me and I let myself drop into its arms.

DREW

S hae remains in her room for the rest of the day and I keep myself busy with work. I've been absent for longer than I had intended, and my backlog is mountainous. The pull to go to her is tidal though, and I stop outside her bedroom several times to check if she's awake. Each time, there isn't any sound of movement. Now, unable to sleep, I climb out of bed and press my ear to her door again.

I'm relieved she's safe and here with me, but my body aches for her. We should be sleeping together at least, with her in my arms to reassure her, but Jamison suggested that she needed her space, and he's right. Shae has said as much—she needs time to adjust and she wants nothing but friendship from me.

I long to open her bedroom door and check on her, to watch her sleep, even. But that seems creepy and inappropriate. Instead, I march downstairs to the gym and take my frustration out on a punching bag.

I can't let you go. How can you let me go?

My heart cracks a little more.

I tell myself half the reason is she's feeling vulnerable and overwhelmed. She needs to adjust to this new self-image before she can be normal with me.

In the middle of the night I'm woken by the ping of a text.

You need to pay. I'm coming to collect.

The number is blocked. I immediately think of Brett. But this is more prone to be some crazy who hates me and my company, and I should pass it onto the police to investigate. Why would Brett say that? What's he going to do—fight me for Shae? I doubt she'd take kindly to us fighting over her. I hadn't revealed how he hit George either, half because I didn't want to scare her since she'd been hanging out with a guy who could do something so violent and it seemed as if I was point-scoring. The other reason was because she has enough on her plate without having to deal with that. I dismiss the thought that the text could be from Eddie. Jeez, it feels like half the world hates me.

By ten the next morning, I decide it's time to check on Shae. She remained alone in her room since early yesterday. What if she bumped into something and hurt herself, or she's stranded in the shower, or slipped over the balcony? The last thought has me rushing up the stairs and listening at her door.

There is only silence.

She's stayed in there for nearly twenty-four hours, though. I knock loudly then speak through the door. "Shae. It's Drew. Time for breakfast."

There's no response. Worried, I peek inside. Shae is lying in bed, facing away from me. The room is freezing, so I go in and close the French doors. When I return to Shae, her eyes are open and glassy, staring at nothing. Tears have created tracks along her cheeks, some dried, others still damp.

I put my arms around her. "Shae, don't cry. It's going to be okay."

Her body shudders and I tug her to me and kiss her neck.

I realize she's naked. A rush of desire makes me harden, my jeans painfully constricting me. I pull in a shuddery breath and rock her. Over her shoulder, I spot a glassy gem on her bedside table, similar to the one I found on my desk when I first reunited with my father. There are some in the White Room, too. I don't remember my mother decorating with them. Maybe Jamison took a liking to them. He often adds new cushions and vases or replaces a faded rug to keep the house up to date.

When Shae calms, she tugs the covers up to her chin. I grin through my worry for her and say, "You're killing me here... knowing what's under there and I'm not allowed to touch."

"I couldn't find the wardrobe."

That wipes the grin away. "Jeez. Sorry. I should've put some clothes out for you." I count the steps to the cupboard to fetch her something to wear. "If you start from the end of the bed and face left, it's fifteen paces."

"This room is huge."

I browse over the area and wonder if it'd be better for her to stay in a smaller room, a smaller home. "I made sure Jamison got loads of shorts and tank tops, but it's a bit cold for them at the moment. Will jeans and a sweater do?"

"Anything," she mumbles.

"I'll put them on the bed and leave you to dress. But I'll be right outside to help you downstairs. Bring your cane. You need to start using it for when I'm not here."

I wait for a reply, but she doesn't even shift.

Walking out the room, I add, "I'm not leaving you here all day. You have five minutes to pull on some clothes, then I'm coming back in, whether you're dressed or not."

"How do I tell if I'm wearing clothes inside out or not? Or back to front."

"Feel for the labels or something." She doesn't move. "Do

you plan to stay there for three months, expecting Jamison to bring you food and drink all day because you can't be bothered to even try?" Of course, Jamison wouldn't mind, but Shae hates to put people out or to be dependent on others.

"I'm not hungry," she says.

"No way, Drew. I'm not doing it." Shae's voice echoes in the cavern-like hallway. "Tell her not to come. I don't want her help. I don't want to be treated as if I'm—"

"Blind?"

Shae bristles. "Don't say that word."

We'd just navigated the stairs and she's as mad as an alley cat because I refused to leave her suite until she got dressed and agreed to come out. I also guilt-tripped her, saying Jamison was sick and couldn't bring her any food or drink today.

"She's on her way already. Listen to me, please. I can't always be here. You've stayed in bed for five days. You can't live in your room for the next few weeks." *Or more.* "You have to learn to get by. If you won't even try to get around the house, then how will you ever go out?"

"I don't need to go out."

The doorbell rings followed by Jamison's alert steps on the marble floor. "May I assume you're ready for your guest?" he asks.

"Yes, Jamison," I say. "But give us a few moments to reach the White Room." I circle Shae in the direction we need to go.

"You should have asked me first, Drew. I'll talk to her today as she's already here, but only today."

"Mr. Vega, Miss Love. This is Miss Tiger," he introduces a petite, casually dressed Asian woman, her dark hair pulled into a thin ponytail.

"Lovely to meet you both." Her shoes squeak with each step. "Shae, I assume?"

"Yes, I'm the invalid."

"Only if you want to be." Miss Tiger is painfully cheerful, but she's exactly what Shae needs. I grimace apologetically. "Don't worry," she adds. "By the end of today, Shae, you'll feel much better because our mood brightens when we can cope independently of others, doesn't it?"

The sound of the tinkling of the rigging can be heard through the open doors. Shae glances toward them.

"Excellent. You've got your shoes off already," Miss Tiger continues. "We must rely on our other senses when we're missing one sense. Let's start in this room. What you need to do is visualize your surroundings, imprint them on your brain so you can see them, if not with your eyes, but with your mind."

"Sorry to interrupt you," I say, "but I have to go to work, Shae. Miss Tiger is going to stay here all day, and Jamison, too."

Shae looks slightly startled for a moment but then settles into her blank expression again. "You said Jamison was sick."

I hate to leave her, but Miss Tiger suggested I make myself scarce to ensure better cooperation from Shae. Besides, I haven't gone into the office for over two weeks and they're getting touchy.

"Later, Mr. Vega," Miss Tiger says. "We can't wait to show you what we learned."

"Please, call me Drew."

"Okey dokey. Bye then. Shae, let's consider all our sensory clues. First, the sense of this carpet under our soles. It's different to the feel of the rug. Come." She moves Shae a pace forward where her foot lifts the edge of a rug and she almost stumbles.

I head into the hallway, check my pocket for my cell, and

pick up the briefcase I'd previously packed. Arnold is waiting in the car and I have four missed calls from Gavin.

When the phone rings again, I answer.

"You're coming in today, Drew?"

Irritated, something snaps inside me. "Yes. I said I was."

"It's important you do this time."

I acknowledge Arnold and climb into the vehicle. "What's going on, Gavin? What's happened?"

Silence follows and I check my phone in case the reception is bad.

"You've been absent a lot, Drew. Firstly, after your father died, and everyone understood that. And we comprehend it wasn't your intention to be kidnapped by Eddie Riley. However, your long absence was noted. Then you got delayed in England—supposedly it's because of the same woman as before... Shae Love?"

"I've explained why though. She's blind, for Christ's sake."

"*I* understand, Drew. But this is business not a romance novel and..." His pause becomes awkward. "There are rumors."

"There are always rumors."

"Some more dangerous than others. These allude to a growing number of both board members and shareholders working toward a vote of no confidence... in you. In addition, Lucas has had some contact with the company directors—"

"What? But he hasn't done the paternity test yet."

"True. But that hasn't stopped him from suggesting that he would make a better CEO than you, ready for when he does prove his claim. He's the CFO of *Olden Holdings*, a big player in the retail and real estate market. Let's just say, people are listening to him."

A memory of a disappointed expression on my father's face hits me. I'm letting him down again. What if I'm responsible for losing the company he spent his life building if

Lucas mounts a hostile takeover? "I'm on my way, Gavin. I won't drop the ball again."

"There's one more thing."

I grip my jaw, trying to remain calm.

"We've failed to stop Lucas from exhuming your father's body."

SHAE

I bang my shins on the table in the White Room and recall how it's as big as a bed.

"I'll do an overview and then we'll go through each room of the house you tend to use, okay?" Miss Tiger's words interrupt my thoughts. She's too cheerful, and I almost roll my eyes. "Tell me, what other sensory clues do we have in this sitting area, Shae?"

"The sound of the yachts, the waves, the birds, the breeze, the lawn mower, and the scent of Mrs. Jones' pumpkin soup for lunch."

"Oh, wow. You *are* good at this. What you need to do is connect those sounds and smells to each room."

I gift her with a smile.

"Rooms also sound different when you speak. Crazy, isn't it? This space will carry your voice differently to the windowless sitting area through there and bathrooms will echo."

We spend the day testing rooms for sensory clues; it's a matter of cataloging them in my mind so I know where I am. She describes the spaces—the ticking clock is on the mantel of a fireplace, but the ticking clock in the hallway has a much deeper 'tocking' sound. The kitchen door is padded while the others are wooden. I step out the distances in the kitchen, counting the paces between destinations by following the sounds of the fridge, a running tap, the dishwasher. We count stairs, find the height of handles and light switches. The hardest skill to learn is 'feeling space'. I'm told I'll begin to sense the space of doorways and windows.

"You'll experience a sense of being closed in because the walls will bounce sounds to you more quickly. But in a large room, sounds aren't as sharp, and they fall away from you. It takes practice, but your visual memory will develop."

After her tutoring, I feel safer and more confident, and slightly less pathetic. Less broken. Less dead inside.

"On Monday, we'll work on tactual sensitivity," she says, "to ensure you don't clean your teeth with an antibiotic cream or put mustard on your food instead of ketchup."

"Farewell, Miss Tiger," Jamison says. I'd heard his footsteps on the marble and knew it was him because he marches with small, quick steps. I hear the front door click shut. "Mr. Vega is home. He's waiting for you in the White Room." I listen to Jamison's shoes squeak as he swivels and treads in the direction of the kitchen.

"Drew?" I call, afraid to move without someone by my side.

"I'm in the White Room," he calls. He wants me to get there on my own. Something in his voice is grave though, rather than teasing.

"You are so transparent," I say, and twist to the sound of his voice. I walk slowly, counting, and note when the marble becomes the brown cord-like carpet of the dark sitting room. Then I count steps away from the sound of the clicking clock on the mantle. The carpet in the White Room is fluffy. I put out a hand to fumble for a sofa and sink into it.

"I'm exhausted," I say.

"I'm impressed. Could you have walked here on your own

this morning?" His footsteps halt and the leather hisses as he slumps onto the sofa opposite me. Then there's the sound of feet huffing from shoes and each shoe thudding onto the rug. I hate that I can't see him, and now he's sitting on the other sofa, so there's no chance of a casual touch or of catching his scent. The thought surprises me.

"Who's paying for Miss Tiger?" I ask. "She's not going to be cheap."

"Don't worry about it."

"I don't want to sponge off you." I hear his long sigh in response.

"Seriously," he says, the grave tone returning to his voice, "money is the least of my problems."

I wait for him to continue, but there's only the tinkling of the rigging outside. I picture him in his suit, as I'd seen him on TV the first time he stood with his father. He resembled a movie star rather than my barefoot backpacker. A sense of longing for him, or us, *the way we were in Samoa and on Sassy*, strikes me across the chest.

Jamison approaches, his shoes clicking abruptly until he hits the carpet. "I have the champagne you requested this morning, sir."

"Thank you. But please take a seat, Jamison. I have something to tell you. It's... it's not good news."

"I'd rather remain standing, if you don't mind, sir."

"Fine. To keep this short, someone is claiming to be the son of my father. He was born a decade before me, but he has documentation to substantiate his claim. He's been awarded the right to... exhume my father's body in order to perform a DNA test."

No one speaks for a few minutes.

"His intention is to prove his right to inherit my father's estate—"

"Where does that leave you if he succeeds?" Jamison's voice is soft and unusually feeble.

"Lucas would inherit half my father's shares in *Vega Corp.*, and he could mount a hostile takeover if he can get enough support. Also... it's complicated because he wasn't named in my father's will, but he could contest it and receive half of everything."

"Where's the honor in digging up a man's grave?" Jamison says. His words tremble with anger. "It's inhumane. Anthony Vega has been laid to rest and that's where he—"

I hear Jamison's quick footsteps retreat, then a door slamming.

"Are you okay, Drew?" I ask.

"I hate seeing Jamison upset. I'd better tell Mrs. Jones to put dinner on hold. I have to go into the office. I'm sorry. The board is worried about my shares potentially being split in half, meaning I would no longer have a controlling share. They've called an emergency meeting."

I can't believe this is how Drew lives these days. No more working behind a bar, volunteering for the dog shelter, no more rebuilding villages, walking everywhere barefoot, or cycling on the beach. The familiar tightening in my belly stretches. We're back to square one where I'm wondering if I can fit into the lifestyle of a billionaire, and he's assuming I can. Do I want Mrs. Jones to cook my meals every day with Jamison constantly appearing as if by magic at my side? I recall the media circus at the airport. I *know* I don't want that. Not even Drew's fortune can buy me an invisibility cloak.

I sense Drew slip farther from me, but I should let it happen—it's inevitable, like watching a sunset fade.

"Have you spoken to Brett since I told you what he did?" he asks, nearing me.

"I don't need to check what you said." I'm conscious of him standing beside me. "I believe you. Brett has it in him to do that. His crush on me is something twisted and possessive."

Drew places his palm on my shoulder. Even his innocent touch sends a tickle of desire through me. "I never left you, Shae. Neither one of us hurt the other—it was all Brett. I never stopped loving you." His voice is gruff and strained with emotion.

"Please, Drew. Don't push me. I can't think of the future. I can't think of an us. Not until I'm me again. If that never happens, then I won't let you compromise your life by staying with me. Besides, you've got to focus on fighting for your inheritance. You don't need me in the picture."

It's the only time I'll ever be glad I'm blind—I don't have to witness Drew's reaction to what my words have done to him.

DREW

I've always compared Shae to a frightened fawn, easily scared off. Now I grasp she's more like a wild horse, objecting to being coaxed and determined to come closer in her own time. I must trust she still loves me and will eventually choose to come to me. When I neared her the other evening, her breath caught in her throat and her toes curled into the rug. I kissed her goodnight on the cheek, and her face reddened all the way to her chest.

Who am I kidding? *My* pulse had skidded hard enough that I had to go for a swim at ten o'clock on a cold winter night.

It's Saturday morning, another week of work over, and I have breakfast brought up to me so I can catch up on more paperwork. I have to admit to falling behind because I'd found it impossible to concentrate this week—my father was exhumed and reburied. I was advised not to attend, as it could be upsetting, but that didn't stop me from imagining it happening. The internet talked of coffins breaking apart, of maggots and skeleton bones shaking loose, and those images haunted me. The funeral director I consulted said it couldn't happen though, given that he hadn't been buried long. It also meant the paternity test could take place and those results would dictate my future.

I've decided to keep office matters separate from Shae, including the Lucas issue—she's got enough on her plate without my baggage. While I work, I listen to footsteps and the muffled sound of voices and feel comforted by Shae's presence. But I won't go out there and crowd her.

It's late morning when I take an economics book into the White Room to read. Jamison has opened the concertina doors. The walls retreat and the outside intrudes and becomes part of the room. Shae is on a sofa, her feet up, listening to her iPhone through ear buds. She probably didn't hear me come in.

I pluck a bud from her ear and she jumps, grips my elbow as if she's falling.

"Sorry. Didn't mean to make you jump."

"S'okay." She doesn't put the bud back in.

"I decided to do some reading," I add. "I've got a lot to catch up on in the world of economics." I walk past her and sit in the other sofa. "This was my mom's favorite room. We used to call it Mom's Lounge before she died. Dad named it the White Room when it was too hard for either of us to say 'mom'."

Shae pulls her knees up and rests her chin on them, staring into space. Her eyes had once made her easy to read but now they are blank and dead. Maybe it's how she feels inside. I can hear the song she was listening to—something old, from the sixties. She pops the bud back into her ear.

I sprawl on the sofa and we stay there in a comfortable silence until lunch time.

"Are you bored?" I ask while I pass her a plate of sand-wiches. Jamison had deposited a platter on the table for us.

"It's not as if I can go sightseeing." At first, I believe she's making a joke and nearly laugh but then her mouth scrunches and works to straighten. A pebble lodges in my throat and I stop myself from going over to comfort her.

"What about taking a swim? The pool's not far. You could count your strokes so you don't hit the end. Or do breast-stroke. Or simply float."

Shae returns to her ear buds, asking Siri to play an audio book. After she finishes her lunch, she pushes to her feet and slowly makes her way out of the room. I haven't finished my next sandwich before she's back, wearing a white bikini. Her dark hair swirls over her shoulders and across her breasts to her tanned, taut stomach. She takes my breath away.

She suddenly appears uncertain. "I need... someone to help me out there. I need to map it out so I can go independently in the future."

"No problem." I could hug her to me. Instead, I take her hand. "The entrance is a door next to the study. It's a straight passageway, then turn left, and then a couple of stairs. Easy." I lead her forward and count steps with her.

On the poolside, Shae sits on the edge, her feet dangling in the water. She lifts her chin to the sun and smiles up at the sky. It's the first real smile I've seen in weeks. My girl is not an indoor girl. I have to get her outside more. For the next forty-five minutes, she rips up meters in the pool. She's a great swimmer, even doing proper turns at each end. She has no trouble counting strokes and avoids crashing into the wall. Jamison arrives with towels and gives me a nod of approval.

After a while, Shae floats on her back, her arms moving in and out, making snow angels in the water. There's another smile on her lips rather than the blank expression that's been there since the hospital.

She climbs out eventually but lies on her stomach on the poolside. The ache to go to her, to hold and touch her, is like a suppressed scream. I snatch a bottle of sunscreen from the outdoor table setting.

"It may be winter, but you'll still burn. Can I put some sunscreen on your back? I could ask Jamison if you'd prefer..."

She doesn't answer immediately, but then nods. "Okay. Like that day at *The Trench.*"

The day we properly got together. The day she let me kiss her and hold her on the beach. The day I slipped my fingers under her clothes and made her come apart in my hands. As I rub the sunscreen into her skin, I recall every moment and fight with myself not to pull the knot of her bikini as I had that time. Her bikini bottoms had fallen away, and she'd opened her legs to me. She had been hot and slick, and I know she'd feel the same way now, heated by the sun's rays. My body stirs and my need for her swells through me.

Once I finish rubbing in the sunscreen, I put the bottle in her hand to let her do her arms and legs. I have to take a cold shower to avoid the urge to slip my finger under the elastic of her bikini bottoms. "Give me twenty minutes. I'll be back to step out the return route when you're ready."

WHEN SHAE COMES downstairs after her swim, she sits where she was before lunch.

"Hey," I say to ensure she recognizes I'm in the White Room, too.

"Hey, back." Before she picks up her ear buds and gets lost in her audio book again, I notice her toes curl into the carpet.

After an hour, I get up and pat her leg. "Want a soda?" I ask after she taps pause. She smiles and says thank you. "I thought I could read to you?"

"I'm not sure I want to hear *Economics Can Shrink Your Brain.*"

"I've already devoured it—twelve times," I retort. "My dad gave me a list of the top twenty books you should read before you're thirty. I have to admit I skipped *The Joy of Cooking*, but have you read *High Fidelity* by Nick Hornby?" She shrugs. "Give it a go, then? It's light-hearted." She agrees and after fetching the sodas and the book, I plunk on the other end of her sofa so I don't need to shout for her to hear.

I lean against the arm, my legs bent, feet on the sofa facing Shae. I balance the book against my thighs and begin. Shae gradually makes herself more comfortable as she listens and whether she realizes or not, adjusts herself to mirror me. Our feet almost touch.

On Sunday morning, Shae's swimming before anyone's had breakfast. I hear her from my bedroom and peer around the corner of the house where I can spy on half the pool. She swims two more times that day. She only stops to shower, eat, and listen to me read. We settle into our same position on the sofa, facing each other, legs pulled up, toes a few inches apart. She could easily stay in her suite, distance herself from me, but she doesn't. Instead, the White Room gets re-christened for the second time—Shae's Room.

A few days ago, Sienna got in touch to ask how we were doing. She told me how her boyfriend, Blue, was a *Seeing-Eye* dog trainer in Cape Cod and now works for a similar company in the UK. When she asked him if Shae should apply for one, he said it was unlikely she'd be approved as Shae's chances of regaining her sight are high. It might happen anytime in the next few weeks. But watching Shae grow in confidence makes me want to do more to help her find the old Shae. I bask in a new idea and text Sienna.

SHAE

Drew had run from the breakfast table today, shouting goodbye and squeezing my shoulder on the way out to the office. With the front door slammed behind him, the house takes on the atmosphere of a crypt.

I sit in the dining room alone.

The two clocks tick and tock out of sync.

The waves outside make the rigging jingle.

This weekend had been quiet, but it was filled with the peace I craved. I'd stopped worrying about Drew's intentions and settled into enjoying his company as he read to me or watched me swim. Now he's gone, and I feel abandoned.

Last night, I had listened to him strum his guitar while I lay in bed. I'm not sure if he was on his balcony—I have worked out that his room is next to mine—but I'd left the French doors open as usual and it sounded as if he was right there, playing for me, singing for me. I had hugged a pillow in bed, remembering the time he sang to me on the beach in Samoa, wondering if he'd sing the same song again. He hadn't, but I fell asleep to the sound of his strumming.

The doorbell rings and I'm stunned by my hope that it's

Drew, returning even for a moment to pick up something he left behind.

But it's Miss Tiger.

I listen to her advancing stride alongside Jamison's quick steps. "I bumped into Mr. Vega outside," she states. "I understand you've done well with your visualizations and sensory clues."

"It's weird how everyone calls him that instead of Drew. He's only twenty-four."

"Twenty-five, according to Google. So, today, we're going to ensure you don't clean your hands with shampoo or wash your hair with bleach."

She checked him out on Google, but more importantly, I've missed his birthday.

"I'm guessing you smell it first?" I say.

"Okay, smarty pants, let's put you to the test."

I can't tell conditioner and hand soap apart, or mayonnaise and yogurt. She pulls out a random drawer and makes me identify things. I figure out the difference between pens and pencils and my shoes versus someone else's. It's another long day but by the end of it, I feel more in control of my life.

As the air cools, which means the sun is setting, I find myself wondering if Drew will come home for dinner or if he'll work late and eat at the office. He's done a lot of that lately.

When he swings into the White Room, I attempt to regulate the extent of my smile, but I know it takes over my face.

"Hey," he says, and I listen to him huff into the sofa opposite me, pull off his shoes, and lump them onto the rug. "I hear you nearly put yogurt on your sandwiches instead of mayo."

"Have you talked to Miss Tiger?"

"Yup. Said you're her star pupil."

"I doubt it."

"Do you want to meet up with her again?"

"Yes and no. I'm not happy that you have to pay for everything."

"She's not expensive. She does two initial tutorials, and then lets you practice yourself before returning if you need her. We can work it out later. I don't mean to brag, but I won't miss a few hundred bucks. Stop worrying, okay?"

I purse my lips and steeple my fingers and decide not to ask about Lucas's claim on Drew's estate.

"Jeez, I need a beer. You?" I shake my head and sense him pass nearby. When he returns, I smell the yeasty drink. He's followed by the clipping steps of Jamison.

"Sir. You have an unexpected visitor... at the gate." Jamison sounds flustered. "Lucas Cunningham."

I gasp and wish I could see Drew's face. There's a long silence before Drew says, "Ask him to please come in."

"What could he want?" I ask. "Why come here in person?"

"That's what I'd like to find out."

"Do you need me to leave you two alone? You should go into your dad's study."

"No, stay. I want to keep this informal, friendly." But Drew's voice is stiff and hard, and I hear him pace between the sofa and the balcony.

"May I fetch you a drink, Mr. Cunningham," Jamison asks as their footsteps near.

"Thank you, yes. Whiskey and water?"

"Lucas," Drew says, and I hear him march toward the door. "Welcome to my home."

"And mine," Lucas says, a chuckle in his words. "It's nice to meet you, little brother."

"Well, those facts are yet to be determined," Drew says. "Jamison, I'll take one of those whiskeys, too, thanks. Lucas, this is Shae Love, my... very good sailing companion and friend."

I cannot see his response to Drew's introduction. He may have simply nodded at me, but he doesn't greet me.

"I decided I'd deliver the results of the test we're all waiting for in person," he says. "Given their content, I thought it appropriate to convene." There's a sound of shuffling paper. "You'll understand why I referred to you as little brother." He chuckles too loudly. "Little brother standing in rather large shoes. You've certainly bitten off more than you can chew of our father's company."

"What makes you say that?"

"Rumors. But I plan to step in and help, as soon as the appropriate legalities are out of the way."

"You do intend to get involved at *Vega Corp.*?"

"Of course, I do. It's my birthright. I only recently sought out my adoption paperwork and discovered exactly what my birthright is. I believe my experience in the business world fully qualifies me to take over the helm from you. I'm sure you're aware—"

"Yes, I'm aware of your resume. But those are fighting words coming from someone who's just met his new family. Shall we begin on a less controversial topic? Jamison, there you are. Thank you. A toast to..." Drew pauses, "family. I've always wanted a big brother."

There's the clink of ice cubes and the tick of the hall clock.

"I'm afraid I don't share your views on family," Lucas says. "Mine has never done a thing for me. Being abandoned by both your parents can leave a somewhat bitter taste."

"They were both so young—"

"If I was in their shoes, I'd have made different choices. My mother, for instance, comes from a wealthy family. She let pride dictate her decision to cast me aside." There's a moment where it sounds like they both simultaneously sip on their drinks. Irritation rises into my gullet the more I listen to this guy. "But I'm not one to reminisce or blame," Lucas continues. "I'm merely explaining my notion that family means little to me. Friends and colleagues, now they are a different story. Luckily, they can be chosen."

"I'd be happy to tell you all about our father. He was a great man who survived a difficult childhood."

"I've read all I need to know about him." Another awkward pause and I bite back at the words I want to fling at him. "I believe I inherited my brains and acumen from him. I can thank him for that, but little else."

Jamison snorts and clip-clops out of the room toward the kitchen.

"Our father was a good man," Drew says. I can sense he's getting upset. "Although, he wasn't perfect. He made mistakes."

"Me being one of them, is that what you mean?"

I jump to my feet. "Of course, that's not what he means," I say. "Drew is extending the hand of friendship, inviting you into his family, despite your rudeness and your desire to cause chaos at *Vega Corp.* Yet you insist on brushing him off and belittling a father you never met. I'm sorry you were adopted. No doubt you felt abandoned, but is that any reason to treat Drew like he had anything to do with it? This is a shock for him, too. Everybody in this world goes through tough times, but it's not an excuse to become hard-hearted and impolite. I'm sorry, Drew, but it had to be said. I'll leave now."

I attempt to march from the room, but having mis-counted, I walk into the wall beside the door. I step sideways and into the hallway where Jamison takes my elbow and guides me to the staircase.

"Couldn't have said it better myself." He chuckles near my ear. Then he marches to the White Room. "May I show you out, Mr. Cunningham," he says, a smirk in every word.

I'm shaking when I return to my bedroom. I refused to listen to Lucas throw Drew's attempts at friendship in his face. Something protective and animalistic had reared up from deep inside me. Now I'm overwhelmed with the need to go to Drew and simply hold him, comfort him—even show him that I do love him. Everything I felt for him in Samoa crowds into my heart. *I want what we had back*. There must be a compromise and we won't have to live in his Sydney mansion all the time. *If* my eyesight returns, I realize, I want to find a way to have a future together.

DREW COMES into my room again when I'm supposedly sleeping; it must be after midnight. This time, he ventures closer and sits on the carpet, leaning against the bed frame. I work it all out from the sounds and the way the bed jolts slightly with his weight. It's good to have him there, and there's no harm in it. At least he's not pushing himself on me. I listen to his breathing, which becomes more labored. At one point, I think he's crying or trying not to sob, but then there's silence as if he's holding his breath. Then a more normal rate of inhaling and exhaling returns. I realize it's hard for him to have me here—he still loves me and hopes for a future. I picture his profile as he leans against the bed. He smells of beer and sweat more than limes tonight, but I fall asleep content—his presence, though secret, is more of a comfort than sighting Sirius had been in the past.

BRETT

I scrutinize the balcony I just climbed down from. Drew and I had done that many times as boys, and the fact that the trees have grown helps my ascent and descent. It's convenient of Shae to leave her French doors open. I don't even have to use my key to gain entry and sneak through the house, potentially risking bumping into someone.

Creeping along the side of the house, I slip past the pool and through the hole in the hedge Drew and I made a decade ago. I chuck the sticky hanky I used to get off with in the bins lined up on the road and saunter to my car parked on the next street. When I'm in Shae's bedroom, I have to jerk off to stop myself from sticking my tongue between her legs while she sleeps.

The sea glass jiggles in my pocket. Having given Shae two of them already, I have five pieces left. I leave Shae a gift after each visit. When they run out, maybe my gift to her can be me and the pleasure I can bestow on her tight little body. I noted her door locks from the inside. And just in case, I added a tracker to her cell phone and recorded her number.

But making her body mine is not going to make her mine for keeps. I want more than a few moments of pulse-racing pleasure. It's Shae's love I need. If someone like her can love me, I can be healed of the past. The nightmares will go, the flashbacks, the feelings which won't leave me alone. I inspect my prosthetic pinkie finger—pathetic and weak, like me. One day, Shae will come to me and willingly spread those lovely tan legs. I imagine her, her head thrown back as I devour her flower. The image makes me impatient.

"After I've given you my last five pieces of sea glass, gorgeous Shae," I say aloud, to make it official, "I'll be ready to put my plan into action. Then we can be together."

Forever.

DREW

After Jamison led Lucas out, I slumped into the sofa and laughed through tears of both sadness and happiness. How bittersweet to have my half-brother turn out to be an ass who hates my family, just as Shae steps up to defend my family, the one she hadn't felt she could be a part of.

Jamison returns with a stern set to his mouth, yet his eyes twinkle with mirth. "Mr. Cunningham needs to learn some manners."

"He doesn't resemble my father or me. Can these tests be wrong?" I trace over the results again. "I'm going to fight it."

"I'm afraid I have a confession," Jamison says. The twinkle has vanished. "He's telling the truth, unfortunately."

"Take a seat, Jamison. You're giving me a cricked neck."

He perches on the sofa adjacent to me. "Years ago, your father informed me of a son he was too young and scared to take responsibility for. He was just a boy himself and was supporting his mother since his father was still in jail. He refused to beg Rebecca's parents for their financial aid. Later, when he had the means to provide for Lucas, he railed over what to do. We had a few long chats, though your father never revealed his name.

Anthony decided to leave things be, not wanting to potentially disrupt his son's life when he was probably a healthy, loved boy. He decided it must be Lucas's decision to search for him. Then he would welcome him with open arms."

"Why didn't you say anything before?"

"I guess I hoped this wasn't that boy and he'd disappear like so many of the other claimants have. But he's the spit of his mother, Rebecca."

"You knew her?"

"No. But she was in the media. She *was* the wife of a celebrity lawyer, after all."

"How come she and my dad split up?"

"I believe the strain of the pregnancy and the adoption, the whole situation, was too much for their young selves to deal with. They argued, and the relationship ended."

"Do you know why Rebecca abandoned Brett when he was a baby? Did it have anything to do with Lucas... or my dad?"

"Your father did confide in me. Apparently, giving birth to Brett reminded her of the son she had abandoned. She couldn't live with herself. Having Brett made her feel more guilty every day. In addition, she was still in love with Anthony, but he had met your mother by then... and Rebecca's husband at the time—Brett's father—uncovered her earlier relationship with Anthony and believed they were continuing their affair. He didn't even believe Brett was his child until Brett lost his white blond hair and turned dark, like him and Rebecca. A quirk of genetics."

"She ran away, rather than face her responsibilities. Had she stayed, everything that happened to Brett after she left might not have transpired. He might've become a different person." I'm back to feeling a little sorry for him. "And it explains why our dads never got on. Any more of Dad's skeletons in the closet you're keeping from me?"

129

"Not that I can recall at this time." Jamison's gives me a fond smile. "Wasn't Shae spot on?"

"She took the words right out of my mouth." I wanted to grab her and kiss her hard. I have the urge to go to her now and simply be with her, but she won't let me near her, and I promised myself I'd remain patient and wait for her to come to me.

"Jamison?" I say. "Lucas is a son Dad would've been proud of—not his rude manner—but he's a successful businessman. He's what my father wanted me to become. If you say my father intended to open his arms to his son should he come looking for him, then maybe I need to do that."

"Your intentions are honorable, sir. Though I doubt your half-brother deserves them."

Before I go upstairs, I visit my father's study. I've recently started using the room. As I sit in his huge chair behind the vast desk, the sense I'm a child playing at being an adult or like I'm sitting with his ghost dwindles. I stay there for a while, hoping to channel what my father might do, if he was alive.

ANOTHER WEEK GOES by and Shae lets Anthony drive her to a doctor's appointment, which is progress. We slip into a routine of reading, eating, and swimming together when I'm not at the office.

It's late and I've just finished *High Fidelity*. Shae's leaning against the sofa, sleepy and relaxed. I budge my feet so our toes touch. She doesn't react. I leave them there, the blood fizzing through my veins like soda. My phone vibrates. I read the text: it's Finn—he and George will sail *Sassy Jam* to Sydney in eight days. I rap my toes on Shae's to catch her attention.

"Top five foods," I ask. The character in *High Fidelity* spends a lot of time compiling top five lists.

Without hesitation, she reels off six. "Lu'au, taro chips, salted beef, oka, pancakes and jam, pork in coconut sauce."

Each food is one we shared in Samoa or on *Sassy*. I scrutinize her, but there are no clues to help me interpret her answer. Is she opening up to me? Giving me a signal? Every part of me wants to hold her and kiss her silly. But I won't spoil the trust I've built if I'm reading her incorrectly. It's possible they *are* her favorite foods. I get up before I do something I'll regret.

"Just remembered, I've got work to do. See you tomorrow."

I sit alone in my room, confused by how churned up I am. Shae's words suggest she thinks about those times. *Maybe there is hope.*

The next day, Sienna and her boyfriend arrive—part two of my plan to cheer up Shae.

Shae and I are on the deck, taking in the winter sunshine, when Jamison leads them out to join us. Shae turns at the sound of them.

"We have visitors," I tell her as Sienna launches herself at me. I hug her back and nod at Blue, who's holding the leash of a guide dog.

Shae stands, a little worried. "Who?"

"It's me, Sienna, and Blue, my fiancé." Sienna flashes her ring finger at me. "He proposed on the flight. How romantic is that?"

"Hi, Drew. Shae," Blue says, stepping forward. "We bought you a present, Shae. His name's Boomer." He bends to release the leash and guides Boomer toward Shae. The dog sits when asked. "Stroke him. He's a guide dog."

Shae's confusion treks across her face but she allows Blue to direct her hand to Boomer. She pats him, a fake smile pinned in place. I'm confused myself, because I remember she was fine with dogs in Samoa. Now, she looks as if she might cry.

I rub Boomer's back, ignoring the awkward silence. "Hey," I whisper near Shae's ear. "Are you okay?"

Her mouth twists. "I'm sorry. It's just—" Then she bursts into tears.

I wrap my arms around her, mouthing "sorry" to Sienna and Blue, who are holding hands and baffled.

"Are those tears of happiness, Shae?" Sienna asks.

Shae snort-laughs. "White sticks and guide dogs mean… They confirm I'm blind."

"Temporarily," I assure her. "He's meant to provide you with some company while I'm at work, and you can go out without me to escort you. He'll give you more independence."

"I know. I know. It's just highlighting my… how helpless I am. But you're all amazing. Sorry." She turns to Blue and Sienna. "Did you bring him from England?"

"No. He's Australian-bred," Blue says. "Normally it takes a while to receive a seeing-eye dog and even then, they don't give them out to people who aren't declared legally blind. But Drew pulled some strings."

"As did Blue. He's a seeing-eye dog trainer and he has some great contacts," Sienna adds.

"But Drew had the cash," Blue says.

"I made a donation," Drew explains.

"A rather *large* donation."

Shae bends to touch Boomer again, this time squatting to give him a hug. "Sorry, Boomer. It's not you. It's me. You're lovely and soft. What breed is he?"

"A golden retriever," Blue answers. "He's recently finished his training, but I can help you bond and teach you how to instruct him."

"And when your vision returns," Drew says, "you can keep him."

Over the next week, Sienna and Blue stay with us and accompany Shae while I'm at the office. There are endless meetings regarding Lucas with the added worry he may ally with another shareholder and gain a majority stake. I'm grateful Sienna's here to distract Shae and keep her occupied while I'm absent. Blue helps her learn to work with Boomer, and they walk on the beach and even go shopping. Still, the spirit of Shae which has been locked away since her accident remains elusive. Maybe it's too late and it's lost. I just hope not forever.

SHAE

"I don't want to go," I say and leverage myself out of the pool.

"Come on, Shae," Drew says. "It'll be good for you. You need to get out more."

"I've been out plenty with Blue and Sienna." There's a moment of silence. I imagine the three of them exchanging glances and I feel even more separate from them. I wrap the towel around myself and begin to hedge toward the house. But I walk straight into Drew's extended arm. The warmth of him against my cool skin, the nearness of him, has me coming undone, and I ache to wrap myself around him like a towel.

"Hold up." Drew's tone is strident. "Arnold will drop us a hundred meters from the ferry."

"You don't have to use the cane either," Blue says. "You have Boomer to guide you. It's a great idea, Shae."

"You'll be out on the most famous harbor in the world, the wind in your hair," Drew says. "You'll love it." His voice is a low whisper and my insides tremble. He takes my hesitation as a yes. "I'll contact Arnold and change my clothes. Meet in the hall in twenty."

Half an hour later, when we emerge from the car at the ferry terminal, a cacophony of noise bombards me—voices, footfalls, cars, a closed-in sensation, exhaust fumes, cigarette smoke, cell phone ringtones, something sticky under my shoe. I'm on the sidewalk next to Sienna and I freeze. Drew arranges where to pick us up with Arnold and passes me Boomer's leash. I take small steps, walking between the three of them.

"The terminal is fifty meters from here," Sienna says, but her voice sounds as if it's a mile away because my heartbeat crashes in my ears.

They were right, though—being on the ferry is a little similar to sailing on *Sassy*. They guide me up some stairs to the front. I grip a metal bar, shut my eyes, and lift my face to the salty breeze. During the entire half hour trip, I imagine I'm on *Sassy Jam*, alone, sailing into the sunset into a people-less world. Drew, Sienna, and Blue leave me to my memories and everything recedes so I can daydream. Only once do I get a fright when a man knocks into me and then grabs me by the belt loops on my jean shorts to steady me. It seems an overly familiar thing to do. He's so close I can smell the beer he just drank.

"Sorry, gorgeous," the guy says, his voice unusually deep. Normally, I wouldn't be spooked, but being unable to see him or where he goes throws me and I'm back to feeling vulnerable.

When the ferry stops and Drew comes to collect me, he puts an arm around my shoulders and we walk off the ramp together. "Perfect day to be on the water," he says. As our legs brush against each other, a hard shape, possibly his key, presses into my leg.

In Manly, we stay in the ferry terminal and order hot chocolate made with real melted chocolate. Sitting down, something hard presses into my leg again. I put my hand in my pocket to find what feels like a smooth pebble.

Sienna slaps a hand on my arm, and I drop it back into my pocket, unable to think how it got there. "You should've heard Drew on *Karma*, Shae," Sienna says. "He was non-stop, 'On *Sassy Jam* we did this and Shae taught me that, Shae said x, Shae said y.' It was pure torture for all of us."

Drew laughs good-naturedly. I wish more than anything that I could see what's in his eyes, observe his toothpaste commercial smile. *I can't be painted in sunshine anymore.*

On the return ferry trip, I settle in the same spot, my hair flogging behind me. I'm shivering, the early evening wind too cool for a T-shirt and shorts. After a while, I sense someone standing beside me. I clutch the railing, certain it's the same guy who crashed into me earlier.

"You're cold, but happy." It's Drew's voice.

I release my grip on the pole. "I always imagine Australia as permanently hot. Bit unprepared."

He rubs my arms with his palms. "You're freezing." He circles my waist, his warm chest against my cool back. I stiffen.

"Would you rather go inside?" His breath on my ear sends a sharp tremor through me.

I shake my head and let myself soften against him.

"I'll just keep you warm," he says, and I silently add, *and safe*, mimicking what he said to me the first time we slept on the beach in Samoa.

I PERCH on my bed and listen to Sienna admiring the size of my bedroom, the amazing views, the thick pile of the carpet, the painting above my headboard.

"Ooh, what are these?" she exclaims.

"What are what?" I bend to stroke Boomer, who's madly sniffing at something on the carpet where Drew usually sits on his secret nocturnal visits.

"Sorry. They're like green and blue gems, all in different shapes. They catch the light prettily. One of them has a tiny hole drilled into it. I wonder if it's sea glass."

"I didn't know they were there."

"Here. Touch them." One by one, she puts five cool stones into my palm. I rub their smooth surfaces with my thumbs until they warm up. They remind me of the sea glass I collected for George for his wind chime. I should ask him if he's made it.

"I found a similar one earlier today, it seems." I pull the pebble from my pocket. "Are they in a bowl for decoration or something?" I must've absentmindedly slipped one in my pocket.

"No. Just in a neat circle on the nightstand. Anyway, I'll say cheerio, Shae," Sienna says. "Thanks for having us, and please don't get up in the morning. We're leaving at stupid-o'clock and Arnold is driving us."

"Thanks for coming. Blue's amazing. Good luck with everything in England."

"Drew's a special guy, too, Shae. Don't keep pushing him away. One day, he might *stay* away."

"It's not that I'm pushing him away. I'm protecting him. And myself. Every time we find each other, the universe creates a situation which pulls us apart. What if it's trying to tell me I don't deserve him?"

"They say we accept the love we think we deserve. According to Jamison. I thought it was profound. He's a wise man."

"I think that was originally in The Perks of Being a Wall-flower. They also say girls marry their fathers."

"When Finn and I were together, he shared memories of your father with me. Drew isn't like your dad. Believe me, Drew's one of the good guys. When you almost die together, as we did on *Karma*, you learn what people are made of."

I remember when Drew and I were thrown overboard,

and we nearly died. I had learned how love can be empowering.

"From what I've seen and heard, you and Drew are meant to be. Jeez, if you'd seen him on *Karma*. He was one-tracked —sniffing apples and staring at the stars like you might be up there. When anyone asked about you, he'd get this ridiculous puppy dog expression. There's no doubt Drew loves you."

That night, I toss and turn, going over Sienna's words regarding keeping Drew at a distance and accepting the love we deserve. He visits my room again, and I struggle to remain motionless and not lean over and stroke his hair, even beckon him into bed with me. Again, his breathing becomes erratic—maybe he's upset—then it stalls in his throat and dies away. I'm supposedly protecting him from getting hurt, yet here he is, barred from touching me because I asked him not to push me. He's sitting by my bed and horribly hurt… because this is the closest that he can get to me.

"Drew?" I whisper, wondering why he washes away his lime scent at night.

He seems to hold his breath. Is he too upset to speak? Or worried I've busted him. I almost reach for him to comfort him. But what might it lead to? Already, I'm wet for him. Am I ready for sex? How do blind people make love? Of course, they can, but… it's like my first time all over again.

Focusing on his steady breathing, I let myself recall intimate moments we've shared and imagine doing them again, but without being able to see. The more I remember how his kisses melted my insides to slush, how his touch set my body on fire, how resting in his arms felt safe, the more the core of me aches for him. My breaths turn erratic.

"I *do* want to be with you," I say. I'm on the verge of reaching for him when I sense him moving away from the bed. His footsteps are muffled by the carpet and he's so quiet with the door, I don't hear it click. The room is silent and I'm alone again.

Why didn't he say anything back?

I roll onto my side and stare into the space where he was until my eyelids can't stay open. He could've easily slipped into bed with me—surely, my words could be considered an invitation. But he's a good guy, as everyone says, and he's giving me the time I asked for.

I dream of tumbling through the never-ending darkness, of the darkness becoming something thick like blood, and closing in on me, choking me. I clutch around to catch hold of anything to halt my fall, but I only drop faster. My scream pierces the dark and I believe as long as I can scream, I am alive and someone might help me, so I mustn't stop.

Then Drew's there, gripping my shoulders, repeating my name.

"It's okay, I'm here. You've had a nightmare," Drew says. My breaths are sharp and fast. He pulls me to him and rocks me, stroking my hair until I'm calm.

Drew then helps me untangle the sheets and lie down. "You have these blue and green gems in your room, too," Drew comments as he tucks me in. "Jamison has no idea where they came from. I have one in my bedroom and there's another on the table in the White Room. They appear out of thin air. You have seven of them. You must be especially magical."

"You can have them."

"That's okay." He sits next to me on the bed. "Would you like to talk about the nightmare? Sometimes it helps."

"It was silly."

"Nightmares generally are."

I'm embarrassed about telling him earlier that I *do* want to be with him because he didn't answer. It's possible he believed it was the start of another discussion about how I need to wait until my sight returns. I should be clearer about what I want now.

"I'll let you get back to sleep then," he says, soft. The bed shifts as he stands. "Will you be okay?"

I take a deep breath. "No." Swallowing hard, I add, "Stay with me? I just want to be held."

It goes quiet until he climbs onto the bed on the opposite side as me. He reaches for me and I'm in his arms, taking in the lime smell of him. It's familiar, more familiar than anywhere I've been in the last few months, like how I imagine it feels to return to a home you love. I've never had one of those. I nuzzle closer and the breath trickles from my throat and my body loosens. With every moment, desire ricochets through me. I shift again and take in his hardness against my leg. I nip at his chin. I'm not sure if I was aiming for his chin or his mouth, but it feels good and I do it again.

He turns so his forehead is against mine. Our noses brush. His breath is on my lips. I push my lips to his, and he opens to me, his tongue urgent and hard as our mouths join and move together. My palms glide under his T-shirt and up his back, and he rolls me on top of him, belly to belly. His hands rush under my cropped tank top to stroke my shoulder blades and down again to rest on my hips. He slides me over his erection and we both gasp into each other's mouths. I arch to push against him from a better angle and he yanks my tank up and over my head, lifts his face to tease my nipples with his tongue. I spread my legs and rub myself against the length of him through his boxers and my panties. With each gentle bite of my nipple, a zing of electricity rushes to the core of me until I'm panting with the intensity of it. The orgasm builds slowly, a rising sun emerging from behind the hills, until it bursts through me like the bright light of dawn.

When I collapse onto Drew, I realize I hadn't thought about being blind once. People often make love without the lights on. Why was I worried? Except, I've discovered blindness is more potent than being in a dark room where there's usually a light source, even if it's only the moon. If anything, the utter darkness ensures the ecstasy is more intense, the focus on sensation and nothing else.

I roll off Drew, bringing him with me, and reach for his erection.

"I don't have any condoms." His voice is gentle, gravelly. "It's not as if I've needed any since I got home from Samoa, and it's one thing I'm not asking Jamison to buy."

"I don't blame you." I smother a giggle because the sound surprises me. But I don't stop stroking him and slip my fingers into his shorts. His body tenses and he leans in to kiss me. I move my hand to grip him. His tongue probes harder and deeper until he pulls his mouth away and throws back his head, grunting and thrusting himself into my hand. With my lips against his cheek, I say, "I guess I didn't just want to be held."

DREW

"I've got a surprise for you," I say as we finish breakfast on the deck the next morning. "But you need to have a sweater with you."

"It's Friday. Haven't you got work?" Shae asks.

"Taking the day off."

"Why? What's happening?"

"It's a surprise. I can't tell you. That's the definition of a surprise. I'll meet you in the White Room in ten." I leave before she can pry anything more from me. Upstairs, I text Finn. **On our way in 10.**

Shae hasn't mentioned us sleeping together, so I follow her lead. Being together had been bone-meltingly perfect, but when I woke in the stark light of dawn and felt her petal-soft skin, all the longing I'd suppressed hustled through me, a hot jungle breeze; I had to leave. Now, it's harder than ever to be near her.

I escort her down to the jetty. She's weirdly quiet and tense. I wonder what's making her edgy. Maybe it's all the stairs. Gripping my elbows, she suddenly stops and turns to me.

"Drew. I need to say this. Last night. We shouldn't have…

I got carried away. I'm still blind. What if my eyesight never… we should go back to being friends—"

"Shh. Let's take one day at a time." My heart tightens with disappointment. "Today, it's the surprise you should focus on. You'll like it. I promise." We navigate another step. "Not far to go."

Sassy Jam is moored at the end of the house's private jetty, and George and Finn stand on the deck waving. I wave, too. Shae keeps walking.

"Hey yup, my little Sirène. Fancy meeting you here." George steps off *Sassy* wearing a T-shirt with a picture of the London Eye on it and a red West Ham United woollen hat.

Shae freezes. "George?"

"Got it in one." He engulfs her. "How you holding up?"

George has a three-inch scar across his temple. Maybe it's where Brett hit him.

"Siren? What are you implying about my sister?" Finn jumps in.

"Finn?" Shae shouts. "What are you two *doing* here?"

"They agreed to bring your birthday present," I say.

Shae frowns but kisses Finn's cheek as he hugs her. His easy smile stretches from ear to ear. "You're six weeks too early," she says.

Finn chuckles. "We'll take it back then."

"It? You mean *you're* not the present?"

I grasp her arm and Finn secures the other. "Keep walking," I say, then stop next to *Sassy*. "Give me your hand." I guide her to rub *Sassy*'s hull.

"A boat?"

"Not any boat. *Sassy Jam*," I add.

I'm not sure what I was expecting but it wasn't stunned silence. Then she jerks her head toward me. "You fixed *Sassy Jam* for me?"

"With the help of George and your brother."

Her eyes fill with tears and she launches her arms around

143

my neck. "Thank you. Thank you," she whispers. She lets me go, kneels, and strokes *Sassy*.

"Come on, sis. Get onboard."

We guide her into *Sassy*. She sits at the helm, her hand on the tiller and grins, apparently lost for words. Then she heads toward the companionway and down the three steps into the cabin. I regard her through a porthole. Her palms trace over the nav station, the galley, the edges of her bunk, the lockers. She moves through to the head and the storage areas.

When she comes back on deck, her mood is bright. "I'm so familiar with her, being unable to see is less of an issue than I thought. This is the best present ever. How do I thank you all?"

"Be happy," I say. "It's what we all hope for." Finn and George join in with their agreement. "I've got a guy coming tomorrow to fit some instruments which will help you sail her—including an auditory compass, a talking GPS, and electric winches."

"She's already been fitted with an autopilot and a brand-new comms system," Finn adds.

Shae's face has creased into a frown and she slowly shakes her head. "You're not expecting me to sail her while I can't see, are you?"

"Why not?" George asks. "I have a blind friend who does it better than I do."

"How is it possible? What if I hit someone? I love how you've fixed up *Sassy* and brought her here to me, but I can't sail her." Shae moves to climb onto the jetty. "Can we go back to the house now?" Her foot slips on the wet bench seat and the three of us jump to steady her. She drops into the cramped cockpit. "That's why I cannot sail her. I'm a useless invalid."

"That's absolutely not true, Shae," I say. "You're far from useless."

"You don't believe my sight will return, do you?" She spits the words at me.

"You're wrong. What I do know is your recovery could take months and sailing will help you through a difficult time."

"How exactly can I sail? I'll fall overboard, get knocked out, I can't see the sails, I can't use the instruments—it'll make me feel worse than useless."

"Calm down, girl." George places his hands on her shoulders and pushes her to sit on the bench seat. "Everyone, calm down and listen."

I'd never heard George sound or appear this stern, like a father disciplining his children.

"If I didn't know you could do this, would I have sailed to Australia, girl?" Shae simply stares ahead. Her mouth is set in such a way, I grasp she's seething inside. "You need a boat you're familiar with, true—bu' that's why you have *Sassy*. If the weather's not perfect, you'll stay in the cockpit and have someone else on board. But basically, in calm conditions, you can solo sail her with instruments made to help you—like Drew said. Tha', and learning to use your senses, and you'll be as good as any sailor out there. Bu' it will come with time and patience. In the meantime, you can helm her with a crew."

Shae rubs her brow.

"Figured you'd be right up for this," Finn says. "What happened to your adventurous spirit? Weren't you the sister who crossed the Pacific in the middle of cyclone season? Or was that a different fearless sister of mine?" Finn sits on the cabin roof, jigging his leg.

Shae turns in his direction. "That was your *sighted* sister."

"We're here to help you," I say, stopping myself from reaching for her after her words on the jetty stairs. "Remember how quickly you picked up everything Miss

145

Tiger taught you, and how easy it was to learn how to work with Boomer?"

After a long silence she turns to George. "Maybe take me sailing first and I'll think about it." She breaks into a smile and everyone cheers.

We motor into the harbor and take Shae for a sail as a passenger. George mans the helm and Finn and I act as crew. There's a nineteen-knot wind so George puts *Sassy Jam* through her paces, and we tear up some waves. By the end of the afternoon, Shae has a grin permanently fixed to her face.

———

THAT NIGHT, Shae is talkative and relaxed with her brother and George, and everyone drinks a potful. Excitement pulses through the air like a new beginning.

It's after midnight when Jamison clears the dinner table. He and Mrs. Jones are in their element with a tableful of celebrating people to nurture. There hasn't been enough laughter in this house lately.

Finn and George go for a swim, but Shae insists the water's too cold without the sunshine on her.

"Fixing *Sassy Jam* for me..." she says as we walk into the White Room. "How do I thank you? She's the best birthday present ever. I've tried to figure out how to reclaim her for months."

"Glad she's made you happy," I say. "You'll waltz *Sassy* up and down the Australian coast in no time."

Shae sits in her usual spot on the sofa and encourages Boomer over. "Speaking of birthdays, you kept your birthday a secret. When was it?"

"Somewhere between an English hospital and Australia. It doesn't matter. I had you with me as my present. More fizz?"

"No. Thanks. Better not." Boomer places his chin on her leg.

"Back in a moment," I say and then go ask Jamison for coffee and blankets before fetching my guitar. When I return to Shae, she's listening to the rowdy sounds of Finn and George, a grin tickling her lips. She rubs her hands up and down her arms to warm up and I pass her a blanket before plunking next to her.

I strum the first chords of *I Want Candy*. Shae joins in at the chorus and all I can think is *I want you.* I go straight into *Walking on Sunshine* and the racket brings Finn and George in. They fetch some beers for themselves and sing along. Finn is wired and dances around the room, a cat on heat, making Boomer bark. George splays his body across a sofa, legs apart, arms wide, as if lying on a double bed.

Shae's on the sofa and sitting in the position she usually does when I read to her. I shift to face her and strum Stevie Wonder's *I believe—when I fall in love it will be forever.* I let my bare feet cover Shae's. She doesn't remove her feet and I sing to her whether she knows I'm looking at her or not. I channel everything I feel for her through my toes and will her to feel something in return.

"Okay, lover boy, a more upbeat tune," Finn demands when I finish. I redden and toss a bottle top at him, which he somehow catches and tosses back.

"Nope, I'm for bed," George slurs, struggling to his feet.

"You sure you won't stay in the house, George?" I check.

"Much happier on the boa', thanks."

Finn is to take the twin bedroom. I'm not ready to let anyone sleep in Dad's room yet. George shoves the empty beer bottles into a neat circle on the table, then pushes the bottle tops into a pile for easy clearing up. Little does he know that Jamison won't go to bed until the place is immaculate again. The thought makes me pack up, too, so we can let Jamison go to bed.

"I better fetch my bag off *Sassy*," Finn says, following George. "I might visit Colbie for a while, too."

147

"Don't slip and fall in the water," Shae warns jokily.

She turns on her senses so she can exit the room without tripping. When she reaches the stairs, I walk up with her. Our arms brush and she links hers through mine.

Staring ahead, she smiles. "Great evening."

I lead her to her bedroom door, open it, and stand aside.

She gazes in my direction. "Night."

I bend to kiss her cheek and hold my lips there a moment too long. But she doesn't move away.

"Night." My body is pulsing, a struck gong.

She turns her face to me, and we breathe in each other's air. It would be easy to adjust an inch and kiss her mouth, but I don't want to ruin anything, and I can't bear for her to reject me. Instead, I add, "Your hair's getting very long, like when I first met you." I wind a strand of it through my fingers then place my lips on her forehead before heading to my bedroom.

SHAE

I shut my bedroom door and lean against it, my pulse flashing. He's getting to me. When he rested his bare feet on mine and sang that song, it was as if he was reciting the words of a spell—every part of me opened up to him. One of the lyrics was about feeding empty souls. That's how it felt... like he was feeding my soul.

But worse, as I listened to his voice, I understood his confusion, his longing, his hurt—the hurt *I* am inflicting. Am I doing the wounding when all this time I'm worried I'll be the one who gets wounded?

When we came upstairs, I sought to somehow apologize, to vanquish the hurt. But I didn't know how to without making it worse. I nearly told him I want him, and I need him. But everything is still dark and making promises for a future seems selfish. If my sight never returns, he's the kind of man who'll say he'll stay with me, but after a while, he'll regret it. He'll feel obligated to me. Until I can see again, it would be wrong to get in deeper than we already are.

Breakfast the next morning is eventful with George stumbling in late with a shocking hangover and Finn's room unslept in. He'd met up with Colbie last night for old time's sake.

"*Sassy* and I had a little party," George admits. I listen to him empty his pockets onto the wooden table as he has before every meal since he arrived. From memory, they're always stuffed with tools or a ball of wire and surf wax.

Finn arrives at nine a.m. as George pours a third cup of tea.

"Wearing the same clothes as last night," Drew says, his tone teasing. "Good night out, Finn? Can I lend you a comb?"

"The best, mate. Went clubbing, crashed at Colbie's. She's something else." I hear him pull in a chair and rap his fingers against the table. "Some drunk blokes started fighting and she was right in there, breaking it up."

"You young'uns. It's all different these days," George joins in. His knife and fork scrape on the plate and he talks with his mouth full.

"Brody called," Finn says. "I'll need to return home soon. Mom's having a bad time."

"Is this wha' you mentioned on the trip over?" asks George.

"Yep. Her depression."

George grunts. "Did I ever tell you about my daugh'er?"

"A bit. Fiona?" I say. "She passed away a few years ago—my age."

"Yep. Died because of a guy called Shaun. She said he suffered from depression, and it can be a difficult medical condition, but it wasn't depression. That was an excuse for the abuse." Each time George has mentioned his daughter's early death, he's become morose and gone somewhere deep inside himself.

"They're putting something in the water these days. Violence everywhere. Shaun started hitting her after they moved in together." George's tone is strident. "It was a jealous rage. Apparently, it's a good reason to kill someone you're supposedly in love with. Jus' took her life away. That's why I left for Samoa, else I'd be in jail as soon as they le' him out… I'd 'ave killed him."

I'm shocked by his sudden forthright mood. He's never spoken about his daughter in detail before or sounded quite so angry. It's possible he's still a little drunk. He must've continued his party into the early hours of the morning. I listen harder, and he's slurring his words.

"I'm telling you this because he worries me—Brett does," George continues. "Drew told me wha' he did to split you up, Shae. The lad always concerned me. He's the type who's capable of doing anything—he has no boundaries." There's something wild behind George's words, something not even he can control. "I see Shaun in Brett. One day he's a pussy cat and you think he's nice to have around, the next he's a prowling tiger. Believe me, Shae, Brett could be like Shaun. If he sees you and Drew together, who knows wha' he could do."

Koala bear Brett and grizzly bear Brett. I'd never told anyone about the night he got hold of my gun.

"Shae, you can't see my scar, bu' after you took off on *Ariel* to find Drew and Finn, Brett clouted me over the head with a lamp and knocked me out. No reason, other than he went into a rage because you left him behind. He put me in hospital for days."

"Oh, George. I'm so sorry." Prickles of ice run up my spine. "I brought him into your life."

"S'not your fault. I figured he'd stolen stuff to fund his drugs and booze, bu' the only thing missing when I go' home was the pile of sea glass you collected for my wind chime. He didn't even take the cash from my wallet. Please stay clear of him, Shae. I'm telling you this because I'd hate myself if I didn't warn you. Don't ever trust him. Listen to my warning this time."

Everyone's silent. The clock in the hall tocks steadily. A house phone rings.

"Pass the teapo' would you, Finn?" George adds.

"You and Jamison will hit it off," Drew says. "Tea's always brewing in his kitchen."

As if on cue, Jamison's quick footsteps approach. "Phone call, sir. Shall I take a message as you're at breakfast?"

"Who is it on a Sunday morning, Jamison?"

He doesn't answer for a while. Then I catch Jamison's whispered, "*Brett Abspoel.*"

DREW

Fifteen minutes later, I excuse myself from the breakfast table and find Jamison. In dad's study, I tell him what Brett did to George, adding to the list of wrongdoings of my once best mate.

"First thing tomorrow, let's change this home number," I add.

"Very good, sir. First thing." His expression is full of questions.

"When I confronted Brett at UCLA, I didn't know what he was capable of. He could've put *me* in hospital, too. George's words stink of the truth, Jamison. Brett is a loose cannon. He's shown me that over the years, not just with Shae and George, but with the stuff he did at school—shoplifting, fighting, drugs."

"You kept these incidents from me. Why?"

"I was protecting him." I shrug. "Saving him from himself. I've always felt sorry for him."

"Your office forwarded copies of the latest of three threats they received recently, all sent to a public mailbox belonging to the *Vega Corporation*." He pulls some folded paper from his pocket. "I wasn't going to show you—it's not as if you can do anything about it and I didn't want to add to your list of worries. But if this is closer to home… if this is Brett—you need to know."

It's like acting in a crime film—the notes are a handful of words, each made up of pasted on letters cut from newspapers, similar to a ransom note. The first one reads, 'Watch your back', the second, 'Are you watching?' the third, 'I'm watching.'

"The police found no fingerprints," Jamison continues, "and each one was posted from a different place in Australia. They followed the obvious lead of Lucas, and even Eddie, but when neither of those panned out, they were left to conclude it was a prankster. They've recommended a security firm to take extra measures both at home and at the office. But if you think this could be Brett, we need to tell them."

Could Brett sink this low? And is 'watching' all he plans to do?

———

THE NEXT MORNING the police take my statement regarding Brett. I suddenly don't want to leave Shae and feel safer staying behind the walled garden and security gate. I decide to take time off work both for that reason and to be with Shae on her first day of helming *Sassy*. I'm going to have to pull some late nights for the rest of the week, but it'll be worth it.

Before leaving Samoa, George had learned how to teach Shae from his blind friend who's also a sailor. Yesterday, he tested the new equipment, which will help her solo sail through a series of spoken prompts or alarms.

"You must use your other senses and go slower to give you time to react in a situation, like if you're on a collision course with an object or another boat. That's wha' it boils down to," George says as he sits next to Shae on the bench seat. Finn and I are on the cabin roof, giving them space.

"You might believe sailing is a visual pastime, but if you analyze how you sail, it involves your hearing just as much. Remember how you always listen for sounds which shouldn't be there? And *Sassy* talks to you, doesn't she? When you're in the cabin, you know *Sassy*'s going well by the sound of the wa'er against her hull or the slant of her heeling over. When you're helming, you're steering no' only by sight bu' the sensation of the wind on your face. Think about when you're coming off the wind and you sense the boat heel and the sails take the strain—you're sailing the boat based on the pressure you *feel* on the helm and sails."

George shows her the compass and how its beep is quietest when the compass is aligned east-west. Each direction produces a different beep or ding-dong and has a different volume. It'll remain quiet while she's on course but will begin beeping if she veers off course. The other instruments are connected to audible devices. They speak their readings instead of Shae having to see the readings.

I motor *Sassy* out of Vaucluse Bay and then the three of us sail her through the heads while Shae simply sits and listens to the winches, the cleats, the sails, and senses the wind, connecting what's happening to how it feels and sounds. We aim north where craft traffic will be minimal on a Monday morning.

When Shae finally takes the helm, she doesn't appear nervous. I stand behind her, both our hands on the tiller to let her sense it while I steer. As we pick up speed, she leans against me. She adjusts her stance and straightens again but when we heel sharply, she rests into me again for balance.

"Like old times," I say into her ear. "The wind in our faces, together on *Sassy*, the ocean racing past us."

"Thanks for doing this, Drew. I'm amazed at how familiar

this seems, and how I had always listened to what *Sassy* was saying when we sailed. She speaks a language I understand."

"Good to be back at the helm?" I ask.

She turns her face to stop the wind snatching the words from her lips. Her mouth is inches from mine. "The best."

I have to look away.

George eases himself into the cockpit, his knees giving him trouble again. "Have you got a hair tie?" he asks.

Shae raises her wrist where she wears one as a bracelet and ties her hair behind her.

"It's good to put your hair up," George says. "You can learn to steer a perfect course when you learn wha' the wind feels like on your neck and face. Drew's going to le' go. You're the skipper."

Her grasp on the tiller is determined, her expression busy with concentration. She listens to audio voice prompts, to the beeps of the compass, to the sounds of the water as *Sassy*'s hull slices through the waves. I settle next to her, ready to jump in if I need to. At first, she stands, then sits, our legs pressed together. She stands again and it doesn't take long for her to break into a smile, her ponytail whirling behind her. I get the urge to sketch her. I haven't drawn anything in months.

When her confidence improves, she takes on the skipper role naturally and gives orders to Finn and George on the main and jib. She listens to the sounds of their movement and senses how the boat reacts.

"All okay?" I check.

She nods. "I prefer to stand though. I can feel the way *Sassy*'s moving more accurately, and I sense the angles and appreciate the position of the hull in the water better. And I can hear the sail tensions."

I squint against the sharp sunrays to watch her. She doesn't need to squint—all she can see is a uniform black.

SHAE

While I'm sailing, I visualize the ocean like reliving a memory I can hear, feel, smell, and taste. Taking control of *Sassy* grounds me to the extent I know the old Shae is inside me somewhere.

The next morning, Drew has gone to the office before I make it to the breakfast table. Jamison reports he left at six-thirty and would be home late.

Disappointed, I pick at my eggs, but the thought of sailing with Finn and George today soon rouses me. We stay out on the water all day and this time, I do some of the sail work and even navigate through the heads without help. It's not as hard as I believed it might be. It helps that I remember *Sassy* inside and out, and I know her voice. When we were apart, it was her voice I missed—the base sound of her hull as she reached, the clink of her rigging, the way one cleat sticks more than another, how she hums when we're on the right tack. Had it been a different boat, I doubt I'd have learned so quickly.

"How's *Ariel*?" I ask Finn.

"Still up in Townsville. Brody's working on her. Are you saying you want her as well?" he jokes.

Dinner is a sedate affair. Finn carries on with his story about pirates off the African coast. The whole time I can sense the gap—the space—that's there instead of Drew. Miss Tiger said I'd become used to sensing space, but I'm not sure she quite meant that.

Boomer is a comfort, and I love having him. Though I have never seen him, he reminds me of the dog Drew and I rescued in Samoa—his size and the texture of his fur. I feed him titbits from the table, despite Jamison's disapproval.

After dinner, I pull my weary body up the stairs for a shower but snatch up the cell Drew gave me when it rings, hoping it's him.

"Shae?"

An ice-cold hand clutches my gut.

After a few seconds, I raise the phone back to my ear. "Brett? How on earth did you get my number?"

"Are you okay? I miss you. But I'm calling to let you know you should visit your mom. She's not well at all. She needs you."

"My family has nothing to do with you, and I don't have anything to say to you after what you did. Drew told me everything."

"I figured you'd be mad. But you've got to understand my side of things. It's not black and white. Love never is."

My blood boils through my veins. "Did you or didn't you tell Drew that I loved you?"

"Yes, but—"

"Then that's all I need to know. I can't trust you, Brett. You need to back off. You—"

The phone is snatched from my hand mid-sentence.

"Brett? You've had your last warning," Drew spits. "Stay away." Drew drops the cell onto my bed. "How did he get your number?" He sounds angrier than I've ever heard him.

"He wouldn't say. My mom? Brody? He knows she's not

well. He must've got in touch with them. He said I need to visit her. Could he be in Townsville?"

Drew paces the room.

"Can you block him on my phone?" I ask. "I don't want another nasty surprise call."

GEORGE AND FINN sail with me all week. Each day I grow in skills and confidence, but I miss Drew. He's gone before breakfast and home late every night. I start to wonder if he's avoiding me—if it's impossible for him to spend time with me because these emotions are hard to fight. Have I pushed him away once too often, and like Sienna warned, this time he's not coming back? I find myself crying into Boomer's fur.

I decide it's not possible for me to fly to Townsville, so Finn returns home to support our mom. George stays for another two weeks and we sail together every weekday. Each weekend, Drew comes with us. I wish I could see him though, read his eyes, because there's something not right. He's distracted and quieter than normal. I hear him and George urgently murmur on the cabin roof while I helm *Sassy*. I'm doing it alone and they have nothing to do but be my safety eyes. I'm guessing they're talking about me.

On the morning George is due to leave for Samoa, I'm crushed. I walk him out the front door and we rest on the bottom step waiting for Arnold to drive him to the airport. Drew already said goodbye before he left for the office earlier today.

"By the way, when I was sor'ing through your stuff on *Sassy*, I found a gun and ammunition," George says.

"That's odd. I hid it on *Ariel*." Brett had clearly gone through *Ariel's* lockers at some point because he retrieved Drew's drawings—the ones he used to convince Drew I had moved on. Brett must've discovered the gun, too.

George shrugs. "It's locked in *Sassy*'s cockpit locker now. I hope you have a license."

"It belonged to my dad. He'd have done the paperwork, but I guess it'd need updating. I'll talk to Brody."

"Keep practicing. Keep being fearless, Shae. You're lucky to have this se' up with Drew."

"I'm in a bit of a bubble. At some point, I need to leave and tackle the real world." The sound of tires on gravel approaches.

"You can't hide your heart, Shae. From Drew or yourself. Love is wha' keeps the human race going."

"But look what happened to Fiona?"

He stands and pulls me to my feet. "Drew will never be a Shaun." He hugs me to him. "You must see you've go' a good one there." He chuckles. "Stop being so blind."

I half-laugh, half-gasp, then punch his arm, miss, and hit his chest.

"I'm not joking, my little Sirène."

IT HAPPENS when I'm swimming.

I'm counting laps. *Fifty-Nine.* A flash of light, like lightning. I halt mid-stroke and cast around, but everything is black again.

The doctor said I might begin to see streaks of light before my vision returns.

I don't tell anyone in case I imagined it.

But during the next few days, the flashes return, especially at night. I stomp on the hope they spark but can't help feeling excited. It's been almost three months.

Drew is still working long hours and acting distant. He might've concluded he's done all he can for me. He's given me Boomer and *Sassy Jam* and now he's pushing me to move on... because he is.

I've started to spend more time with Jamison and wonder if I should call on Colbie soon. I often eat in the kitchen, rather than alone on the deck or in the White Room. Today, I make my way there to find Jamison accompanied by the waft of roast beef. Boomer, as usual, is at my side.

"Afternoon, Miss Love. Hungry yet?"

"It's Shae, Jamison... Shae."

"You and Drew are cut from the same cloth. Will you be eating here again today?"

"Yes. Drew told me he spent many hours in this kitchen talking to you—or will I be in the way?"

"Not at all. May I join you in a cup of tea?"

I take a seat on the bar stool at the benchtop. "Given we're in your territory, you don't need to ask."

"I'm going to have to teach you a few things regarding the butler/employer relationship."

"I'm not your employer."

"There's a plate of mini rolls in front of you—one's egg, mayo, and salad, one's prosciutto and pickle, one's brie and cranberry."

"Thank you." My fingers knock into a roll. Jamison clatters with something metal, and I recognize the clink of cups and saucers.

"Drew and me..." I start. "He's pulling away. We're in the past. We're just friends now. Therefore, I'm a guest, not your employer."

"You can fool yourselves, but you can't fool me. May I speak freely?"

"That's a pretty scary question. But I guess so." I nibble at the corner of a sandwich.

"I've lived in many people's homes, seen a great many sights, learned a lot through countless experiences, and I am utterly certain you two are not 'just' friends. I can give you examples of why that is the case and not wishful thinking, for I do believe you have a delightful effect on Mr. Vega. But

161

I only need one example and it is this… when you two are together, the room is charged with an essence of calm while at the same time, there's an excited expectation of something wonderful on the verge of happening. Yet, when either one of you is alone, the room has a sense of mourning to it—as if the air has stagnated."

"No one told me you were a poet. That's pretty. But—"

"Don't insult me by denying it, Miss Love. But we needn't discuss it further if you would rather change the subject."

I don't know him enough to work out if he's teasing or being serious. I hear him pour the tea, stir, and place the cup near my plate. Then he pulls out a stool and I assume he's at the bench top with me. I take a bigger bite of my five-star restaurant bread roll, remembering how Drew said on some things, Jamison is not at all pliable.

"Judging by your frown, you're having an extremely solemn thought," he says, interrupting our silence.

"What you say might've been true a couple of weeks ago, but Drew's preoccupied lately. Distant. He leaves early and returns late. I think he's recently decided we're not going to work out."

"Right now, he has a lot on his shoulders. Lucas is potentially mounting a hostile takeover of the *Vega Corporation* and since the media found out, it's turned into a circus. There are also other issues Mr. Vega needs to deal with, but I'm sure they'll reduce soon, and he'll be back to himself."

"It's because I love him that I have to push him away, Jamison. What if my sight never returns?"

"Again, pardon me for saying, but your stoical attitude is admirable in a romantic heroine from a Jane Austen novel, but not the modern world. The real world contains real people with emotions that cannot be turned off because you say so."

"You sound a little mad at me, Jamison."

"I think I am a little. I'm sorry. But it's a horrible waste of happiness I see before me."

"I didn't make it happen though."

"But you've made the decision for both of you as to how this ends."

"We seem destined to remain ships passing in the night. Every time we come together, something comes along to rip us apart."

"The truth is you're afraid to love. Which is shocking because you're Fearless Shae, according to the press. You're the girl who took on the Pacific and defended yourself from a violent man who threatened your life."

My legs kick rhythmically at the bench top and I reach to stroke Boomer. "You're very forthright, Jamison. I thought you were meant to agree with everything the guest says."

"There are times when it's critical *not* to agree." His stool scrapes the floor and he tinkers in the sink with dishes and running water. I finish my food and take the last sip of tea, feeling as if I've been dismissed.

"Love is never one thing or another," Jamison says. His shoes clip closer so he's opposite me again. "It's never all happiness or all sadness. It's the same with sailing, isn't it? Some days, I imagine, are pure joy. The sky is cerulean blue, the breeze is just right, the sunshine warms your skin. Other days it's hard work. You fight the ocean, battle with the wind, you are thrown around and bruised, so wet you could wring yourself out like a towel. But do you stop sailing?"

"Of course not."

"You love sailing therefore you endure the hard days; you rise up to defeat another storm. The good far outweighs the bad and in fact, making it through the tough days makes you a better sailor. It's the same with love. Do you love Drew enough to endure the bad days, to fight through the tough times because the good outweighs the bad? I know Drew loves *you* enough.

"From what I've seen you'll never give up on sailing, even though it's nearly killed you—more than once—and blinded you. Yet you're going to give up on love—on Drew—simply because you fear a broken heart?"

DREW

Lucas enters the conference room having kept the board waiting for twenty minutes. He sets his briefcase down next to the one vacant chair near the middle of the table, but he doesn't sit. Instead, he paces to where I'm sitting at the head of the table, unbuttons his immaculate suit jacket, and stands beside me.

"Hello, Drew." I stand and we shake hands. "Good morning, gentlemen," he addresses the room, then smiles at Elaine, the only woman in the room. "Good morning, Mrs. Arkwright. Thank you, everyone, for convening to meet me. I hope you don't mind if I remain standing. I think better when I can pace."

He's greeted with disapproving silence, which he ignores. I sit back down.

"I'll state straight up it's not my intention to conduct a hostile meeting. I want to show you I'm willing to work *with* you, to build this company and make it even greater than it is. In fact, fighting is never helpful. I've given you the impression I'd fight for my place here, but that's only if I have to. It's my hope you'll hear me out today. Listen to my concepts and strategies for *Vega Corp.'s* future, and then we can move forward in an amicable way while the legalities transpire." Lucas paces as he speaks, capturing eye contact with each person at the table.

"I understand a major concern is that Drew Vega will no longer have a controlling share if he has to split his shares with me. This leaves the company ripe for hostile takeovers from outside parties, not to mention a gamut of other weaknesses which can be exploited. I intend to address this today and then propose some future strategies."

He fetches a laptop from his briefcase and projects a presentation onto the screen.

His knowledge of *Vega Corp.* is in depth and sophisticated, and he proceeds to coax questions and nods of approval from some of my colleagues. In turn, I feel like a naughty child who's snuck into an adult's world and I want to shrink into my chair. I remember how Shae often spoke of wanting an invisibility cloak, and I understand what she means now. I need one, too.

"HOW CAN I RIDE A HORSE? I'll hit a tree." Shae actually giggles.

She's happier these days. It must be the sailing. I wish it was because of *me*. I swallow the last of the bacon from my breakfast plate and take a final swig of orange juice.

"Believe it or not, the horse has eyes and doesn't want to walk into a tree," I reply. "We're not talking racing through the woods at high speed here."

"It sounds dangerous, Drew. Horse riding while blind?"

"I wouldn't let anything happen. But okay, I'll go alone. I simply hoped to spend some time with you. I've been at the office a lot lately."

Shae's smile stalls for a moment, then she turns thoughtful, chewing on her toast. Eventually, she asks, "Where exactly is this riding place?"

"The station Dad had a stake in. I'm expected to visit at least once every six months and it's been longer than that."

"Is this where your dad's accident happened?"

"Yup." The word comes out sharply. The pressure of my position at *Vega Corp.* and the sense I'm failing my father—not only there but by not visiting the station—is getting to me. Despite hardly ever being alone, I'm lonely and isolated. But none of that is Shae's fault.

I soften my tone. "Are you going to eat the poor pancake, or stab it to death?" I push out my chair. "I must get going."

Shae places her cutlery on her plate and stands. "You shouldn't do this on your own. I'll come."

SHAE

The three-hour car ride west is laborious. Drew is on the phone most of the time, apologizing to me in between calls. I can't even appreciate the scenery out the window. Instead, I let my mind return to the conversation I had with Jamison. I'd spent most of my nights re-visiting it. He'd made me view things from a different perspective, as if I was watching my life from the sidelines rather than living in the confusing middle of it. I also remember what George had said, about hiding my heart.

Eventually, we turn into a road full of potholes, which make us bump from side to side. When the car stops, Drew climbs out and multiple men's voices greet him. My nerves are like Mexican jumping beans. *How do you ride a horse when you're blind?*

My door opens. "Come on, Annie Oakley." Drew takes my elbow, helping me climb out of the car. "I have to conduct a quick meeting, half an hour, but the kitchen staff will take care of you and then we'll have the rest of the day."

My spirits fall.

"The meeting is essential. Sorry. It's roughly ten paces to the porch and there are three stairs going up." He treads beside me, his arm around my waist so there's no chance of my tripping. Our jeans rub against each other as we walk. Then my trainers squeak on a smooth floor and Drew's footwear clip-clops until they're muffled by a thin rug. He settles me into a hard, leather sofa. "Back soon."

Even though I can't see a thing, when he leaves, it's as if the sunlight went out of the room.

"Can I offer you a drink?" A girlish voice makes me jump.

"A coffee would be great, thanks."

While she's gone, I listen to the foreign sounds that surround me—horses whinnying, men's voices and laughter, the hammering of nails, a hose washing something down, slow stomping footsteps, a slamming door. It smells weird, not just dusty but there's a sweetness in the air mixed in with manure and cooked cabbage.

"I'll put your drink on the table in front of you." The girl sounds like she's twelve, though I doubt she is. "I have some riding boots for you to try on. Mr. Vega said a size eight." I wonder how he knows my size, then pull off my trainers and fiddle with the boots until they're buckled up.

Drew had given me a sensory wristwatch. I sip my coffee and check the Braille dots. It's twelve thirty when a door opens and the raucous sound of men's voices floods into the lounge. Footfalls beat in all directions and suddenly, Drew's behind the sofa playfully massaging my shoulders to get my attention. "Ready?"

"I'm not sure this is a good idea," I say.

He plonks a helmet onto my head. "Dave's not happy with you riding solo, given you're not an experienced rider. So, we're going tandem."

I'm relieved, and Drew walks me toward the smell of manure and horses. The ground is uneven, but he has me practically pinned to his hip.

"They've picked us a steady, docile old girl," he says.

"Relax and enjoy the sunshine. I remember how you love adventures."

Entirely unsure, I'm soon climbing some mobile steps to more easily mount the horse while Drew is already in the saddle. His hand comes across my stomach and he pulls me into him. Jammed against his crotch, if my heart wasn't doing a pinball impression before, it certainly is now. My T-shirt is cropped, and his palm is on my bare skin. My cheeks flame.

His other arm rubs against my hip as he fiddles with the reigns. "I'll show you some basics, then you can try." The horse takes a step and I suppress a shriek, my head jerking and colliding with Drew's.

"Sorry," I say. We jolt forward again and keep going. "What's her name?"

"Wicked." The word is hot on the back of my neck and heat zigzags through me.

I laugh. "You're kidding." My breathing quickens, but I think it's to do with the sensation of being engulfed by Drew.

He instructs me on how to sit, my posture and leg position. After a while, he releases the arm around my belly and lets me balance alone.

"Have you ever ridden a horse with your eyes shut?" I ask.

"Nope. But I'll give it a go if you like?"

"Not today, thanks."

"Don't worry. I've got them wide open." He chuckles. "You're very brave." His tone becomes intimate. "Now I'll show you how to turn and halt." His hands cover mine as he shows me how to hold the reins and guide the horse to do what I need her to. "Okay, let's start." Drew makes a sound with his tongue and Wicked takes a pace. I lurch backward but straighten myself quickly. There's the clip-clop of hooves as we withdraw from the noise of the house and stables. I take some deep breaths and relax into the saddle to absorb the bumps.

"You're doing great," Drew says.

"Do you know the ranch well?"

"Yup. I used to ride here a lot when I was a kid. Brett often came with me and my family. But until my father and I… visited, I hadn't been back since my mother died. It wasn't until recently I found out Dad owned it."

"Now *you* own it. Was horse riding your mom's thing, then?"

"And my dad's. Though he didn't do much of it after she died."

I listen to the bird calls and notice the breeze in my hair. The aroma of eucalyptus is thick in the air. It's peaceful and I begin to relax. I ask Drew about his week and he rattles off a list of obstacles he had to solve. I sense he needs this time out. I hadn't stopped to consider the responsibility he's had no choice but to take on.

"The threat from Lucas is becoming very real. I may no longer head up *Vega Corp.* and my home may even have to go during the process of splitting assets."

"That's awful. What will you do?"

"Part of me has imposter syndrome. I sometimes think I don't deserve any of this anyway and I don't believe I'm good enough to take over from the great Anthony Vega. But then I want to fight for the company for my father's sake. Except, I wonder if he would oppose Lucas. *Lucas* is the son Dad wanted me to be. Maybe my dad would think *Vega Corp.* is in better hands if Lucas takes control."

"I wish I knew what to say. Have you spoken to Jamison?"

"Not in detail. I need to work out this dilemma on my own. This is between me and my father and my half-brother. Everyone else has a natural bias. Sailing with you has helped me pull my head out of it all though. So, thanks."

I giggle. "Sailing can solve everything but world hunger."

"I'm a member of a club in Sydney and at the end of last year, I clocked up a lot of experience crewing for other boats.

It gave me the right work/life balance. I haven't had enough of that lately, but it seems impossible. Rather than criticize my father as I used to, I sympathize with him—with how he struggled to find the balance."

"Is that how you got involved in financing Australia's challenge for the America's Cup—through your club?"

"Yes. There's another problem to be solved. They need better management on the team. They keep turning to me, but I don't have time to deal with it. But enough about my issues. Let's post a short trot. I'm sure you want to pick up the pace."

His palm is across my stomach again as he pulls me into his lap and grasps the reins. When he says, "Ready?" his lips touch my ear and a shiver trips into my belly and between my thighs. I fight the desire to twist around and hold him— he's having a tough time and there's no one to comfort him.

"This is how you post a trot," he says. The horse takes a few quick steps before Drew's body lifts out of the saddle a touch, then drops down, bringing me with him. We keep moving in an up-down motion and pick up speed. In my dark little world, it's a thrilling sensation, like sailing *Sassy* in the dead of night. I'm safe with Drew's hold on me and whoop with excitement.

When we stop, I'm breathing hard and laughing and there's the sound of a waterfall or a river. Drew releases me and dismounts.

He places his hands on my hips. "Turn side-on and slip off. I've got you." I trust he won't allow me to faceplant from the horse and slide into him. He makes sure I have my feet square on the ground before letting me go and I hear him lead the horse away.

"Are we near a river?" I ask.

"Yup. Want a drink?" He's next to me again and I walk with him toward where the rapids are. I stop scuffing small rocks and dust and sink into grass. "We can hang out here," he says and pulls me down with him. "Gotta get my boots off."

He still hates shoes. "Ew. Got a peg?" I say, holding my nose.

He retaliates by placing a cold soda on the exposed skin where my T-shirt has ridden up.

"There are apples and muffins to eat. Hungry?" I shake my head, take off the helmet, and pull off my boots. I look toward the sound of the river, imagining it in my mind's eye. Drew opens his drink and crunches into an apple beside me. I realize we're in the middle of nowhere, alone.

"How'd you like horse riding, then?" he asks.

"It's the perfect combo—peaceful but when we went fast, exhilarating. It'd be a bit easier if I could see."

He chews for a while longer, taking two more bites. "One day soon," he finally says.

I don't entirely trust myself to believe that the flashes of light I've seen lately are actually there. Except imaginary or not, they're more regular. And sometimes it's not so black inside my head, but more of a dark gray, as if there's a light source sneaking into a dark room. But what if it never improves beyond that?

We lie side by side in the grass and he describes the clouds to me—how one resembles Jamison and another an upside-down Christmas tree. Our arms lightly brush together and every part of me wants him to hold me. Inside, my body buzzes with anticipation. I feel him pull up onto his elbow.

"Good to be out?" he says, his voice low.

I work out he must be hovering over me, and I slowly reach out to stroke his face. He doesn't speak as my fingertips touch his cheek and trace along his jaw to his chin.

"Have you forgotten what I look like?" he asks.

"Of course not." But I keep tracing my fingers up and over his lips as if I'm trying to see him with my fingertips. My gut lurches because I'm knowingly pulling him in; he's a fish on a hook. Desire wades through me, hot and buzzing, and slowly, he comes closer. He touches the edge of his nose to my nose. My breath quickens. There's the sharp rise of his chest as his mouth covers mine. I hold his face, tugging him to me to deepen the kiss. There's a rumble deep in his throat and he fists my hair, urging me to roll on my side. With the sound of the river and the warmth of the sun on my skin, I relax and enjoy the build of heat between my legs and the surge of need for him.

I gasp as he tugs my head gently, exposing my throat. His mouth is hot and soft against my neck and it's like I'm falling, falling into him. I let go and allow myself to fall. Being here with Drew feels exquisitely right. I crush him to me and recognize if we keep going, I'll rip off his clothes. Drew must sense the same thing because he pulls away. Our mouths separate, and we're panting.

Neither of us speak when he tucks me closer, holding me as we listen to the river. Our chests pressed together, the beat of our hearts slows. I take in the sensation of the grass below us, imagine the clouds tripping above us, and I snuggle, my head tucked beneath his chin. We could be on a beach in Samoa or on *Sassy*.

Truly, nothing has changed between us.

In that moment, I no longer doubt I want to be with him. I've grown used to Jamison—to everyone who works at the house—I *like* them even. It's now clear I love Drew enough to ride out this storm with him and to work out how to live with the media attention. I can't leave him. Not again. Not a third time.

My nose bumps Drew's cheek. "Do you still want me, even if I never see again?"

"Yes. Yes. How many times shall I say yes?" His lips brush mine as he speaks.

I crush my mouth to his, hard and needy, sweep my tongue between his teeth, the swell of love and need making

174

me press my body against his. The fight to keep him at a distance, to wait until my sight returns, weakens. It's replaced by a more demanding struggle to fully and freely uncage the love for Drew I have locked away. This fight is not with Connor, the Pacific, the law, or my parents. It's with myself. And it might be the hardest battle yet.

DREW

I've never kissed a girl and felt as if time stopped. I'm giddy with the fact Shae has finally let me close again. *She came to me.* I could sense her desire in her kiss and heard the longing in her voice when she asked me if I still wanted her.

I kiss her like she's mine, not like I'm worried she might reject me at any moment. Eventually, I'm the one who pulls away to stop myself from undressing her on the riverbank. I'm heady with the craving throbbing through me. I want to tell her I love her as much as ever, but I keep things light— she's never said those words back to me, and I won't put any pressure on her.

I need to walk to distract myself. I pull her up with me.

"Come," I say, my throat thick with desire. I place an arm around her to ensure she doesn't stumble, and we wander along the river. I breathe deeply to slow my pulse and when we reach a big, flat rock which edges out over the rapids, I guide Shae to step onto it. I straddle her, keeping her safe from slipping in. Our bare feet dangle over the rapids, a foot above the icy, splashing water. I could do with showering in it.

Breathing in the apple scent of Shae, I mull over the setting sun—full-sized and heavy with reds and oranges, it seems like it's throbbing in the sky. *I wish she could see it.* I describe it to her, along with the river and the countryside surrounding us.

"We could be in Samoa. I have island Drew back," she says.

"You always had island Drew."

"It must be hard." Her voice is slightly above a whisper. "Visiting this station… after your dad's accident."

Dad had been on the edge of my thoughts all day. "It is weird, riding without him—without Mom even. It drives home the idea it's just me now." My arms are around her waist and Shae clasps them. I kiss her temple. "But I'm glad I came. It's as if I'm saying goodbye—saying it at the funeral was too soon, too hard. But it feels right today."

"You've had a tough year, haven't you?"

The best year and the worst year. I observe the sun, sliced in half by the horizon. It oozes oranges and reds across the sky.

"When I was here with my dad, the last time, I didn't know who I was or how everything was going to work out with him. I was afraid I'd made the wrong decision and worried we wouldn't hit it off, and he'd grow impatient or disappointed in me. But now, I get the impression he'd approve of me. Funny how even when we're supposedly adults, we need our parents to approve of us."

"You've done an amazing job stepping into his shoes."

"I don't believe I'll ever fully step into his shoes, but it's coming together." I don't mention how Lucas has already stepped into his shoes better than I have. "But that's all boring stuff. You, on the other hand," I wind a lock of her hair around my finger, "are far more interesting."

Shae turns her face to mine, twists her body for me to find her mouth. I kiss her until the sun sinks and the cool night air blows in. I'm not sure what's going on between us today, if this is some temporary intimacy that will vanish once we return home, but this time I cannot stop myself from touching her. I need to remain intimate and to secure this loving feeling flowing through us.

I compartmentalize everything else but Shae, and bury my face in her hair, nibbling her ear, licking and biting at the skin of her neck and shoulders. As she relaxes in my arms, my fingers loosen her belt and slip inside her jeans. She rests her back and head against my chest and my body cups her as my fingertips dip and nuzzle between her legs. She opens them wider, allowing me more freedom to stroke her.

My free hand slips under her T-shirt and into her bra. She arches into me and pushes her mound against my fingers, a moan skidding from her. I don't rush but take in the texture and taste of her sun-bronzed, smooth skin, the smell of her silky hair when it brushes against me. My hands move slowly, gently, drawing out the moment, and when I nudge my erection against her, I wish I'd brought contraception. The thought of thrusting inside her elicits a groan from me and I nibble at her earlobe, tweak her nipple, and circle my fingers between her legs faster. Her gasps grow louder until she's shuddering and bucking, then waning against me, a flag blowing in the breeze until the wind diminishes.

It's late when we return with the horses, and Arnold is leaning against the car having a smoke. He lifts a hand in greeting, then stubs out the cigarette in the dust.

Squashed up together in the back, Shae's head on my shoulder, Arnold expertly darts through dark, winding country lanes. I think of my father and the last time I left the station and when we hit the motorway, I find myself silently saying *Bye, Dad*. His cowboy hat is in my lap and I grip it to me.

Beside me is a report Dave gave me. Following the declaration my father's death was an accident, Gavin Myers had instigated an investigation and got homicide involved, mainly to cover some sort of insurance and legal issues associated with someone as wealthy and high profile as Anthony Vega dying in a freak accident. I'm keen to read it but refuse to pop the bubble of intimacy around me and Shae.

SHAE

After Arnold drops us home and Drew and I traipse through the front door, Jamison is there to greet us. Drew apologizes for our late return, explaining how it was the perfect day for horse riding, and then he tells Jamison to go to bed. Boomer comes to say hello and nuzzles my legs, then curls into me when I lean down and draw him in.

"I'm afraid I have something urgent to discuss with you, sir," Jamison says. "Perhaps after your shower, we could talk?"

"Sure. I'll take Shae upstairs first."

Disappointment surprises me—I had hoped Drew might sleep with me tonight. I need to press my naked body against him and have him inside me. Today's intimacy cracked the walls around my heart, and I must ensure they don't get rebuilt. I want to stay open to him and to a future with him, but I'm used to my defences rebuilding themselves to protect myself. I'm used to chickening out. George was right—I'm afraid of love.

Even though I'm capable of climbing the stairs without help, Drew holds my hand and takes me up. My belly colly-wobbles.

I gasp as a flash of light surprises me. When I make out the shape of a sloping banister, I stop. Across the hall the electric lights are hazy suns behind thick gray clouds.

"You okay, Shae?" Drew asks, his words laced with concern.

"I can... see something."

"What? What can you see?"

"It's shadowy... but shapes of things, especially the lights."

"Shae, this is brilliant. What a great day. It's all going to be okay."

The stairs appear flat and blurry, but I step up them, gazing around me. "The lights are like lightbulbs in a blizzard." I walk toward my room and once inside, tug open the French doors. Drew is behind me. "There are outlines of masts sticking up. There aren't any details but it's like viewing things in the mist." I twist to Drew and for the first time in three months, I can make out the shape of him. Soon, I'll be able to get lost in his eyes again.

DREW

I go into the kitchen to meet up with Jamison, the report detailing my father's death in my hand. I'm not patient enough to wait until morning to read it. Jamison's not going to have good news as he would never ask me to discuss anything at this time of night unless it was urgent—the evening is spoilt anyway.

Jamison's expression is grim as he passes me a beer.

"What's happened? Lucas? It's Brett, isn't it?"

"Sorry to interrupt your relaxation time, but I felt it pertinent to inform you as soon as possible. We've had another note. This morning. I notified the police and they've already been here. They've added extra security. As have I."

I grip my jaw. My chest constricts. "What did it say?"

"It read, 'It's my turn'. Same cut out newsprint letters. But this time, the note was splattered with droplets of blood—cat's blood, I'm told. And this time it was posted from down the road."

"They can't confirm if it's Brett or not?"

"No. In addition, Lucas is back in the frame."

What does the note mean? "What if it's not Brett or Lucas at all?" I snatch up the beer bottle and drag on it, then pick up the envelope Dave had given me at the ranch. My finger slides under the seal to open it. "This is the report detailing my father's accident. Gavin investigated it after the police decided there was no crime involved."

Sitting on the bar stool, I read and swig at my beer. Jamison tidies and fiddles in the fridge, finding ways to give me my privacy. "The ruling is accidental death," I say, "after the horse got spooked and refused the jump—which we knew already." I read on and my eyes stall over the words *sea glass*. I recall waiting in the Range Rover after the accident, overhearing some of the guys talking. They discussed how some shiny blue and green stones were left in front of the hedge Dad jumped and how they likely startled the horse, a horse who had previously stalled at the glint of sunshine off puddles in the road. "Jamison! It turns out the stones which spooked Dad's horse weren't stones at all. They were sea glass. Jesus. Oh, jeez. *Jesus, no*."

Jamison drops the cup he's drying—it shatters across the kitchen.

"George said the only thing missing after Brett knocked him out with a lamp was the sea glass Shae had collected for a windchime he was making. They had no value. Brett didn't even take the cash in George's wallet." An electrical storm blows through my head and I'm up, pacing the room.

"You believe Brett planted the sea glass to spook the horse?" Jamison's expression is wide-eyed, his skin gray. "Why would he want to harm your father? He's been nothing but good to Brett his whole life. The kidnapping incident—"

The truth is like a freak wave bowling me over. "He hadn't wanted to kill my father." Everything starts fitting together. "He hospitalized George, manipulated Shae, lied to me, threatening me with bloodied notes, threatening Shae's mother. Brett's a loose cannon. He's capable of anything. He needed me out of the way. Brett intended to kill me... so he could have Shae."

The letter flutters to the floor and I race out of the kitchen. "Call the cops, Jamison." I take the stairs three at a time, remembering the blue and green gems on Shae's beside table. I hadn't realized they were sea glass, having never seen any sea glass before, but now I'm sure they are. Brett has a key to this house. Has he come inside? How did he get through security?

Forgetting to knock, I burst into Shae's bedroom. She's not there.

The net curtains billow at the open French doors. I rush onto the balcony, but it's empty.

"Shae? Shae?" I race toward the bathroom door as she opens it.

"What's wrong?" She looks alarmed and she's staring right at me, rather than through me or past me. Relief that she's there relaxes my stance and I take in how amazing it is that her sight is returning. My shouting has wiped the smile from her face though, and I realize I can't reveal my suspicions. Not yet. Not until I'm sure.

"Nothing. I couldn't find you." I wander to her bedside table and pick up the handful of sea glass. I should give them to the police. "Listen, you must shut the French doors at night. For security."

"I guess. But I like the sound of the yachts and the sensation of the breeze and soon, I'll stargaze through them when I lie in bed."

"But close them when you go to sleep, okay?" I lock them. "For me. I want you to be safe."

I'm shaking when she steps toward me and puts her hand on the breastbone above my frantic heart. She places a soft kiss on my lips. "You could stay with me and keep me safe tonight."

I stir and harden, but there's a knock on the door. I almost say, "Not now, Jamison," but remember I asked him to contact the police. I sigh against Shae's lips and move to let him in.

"Sir. I have an urgent phone call for you. You should take it in the study."

I turn to Shae. "Sorry. This never happens. But I won't be long."

Watching her fight to hide her disappointment tugs at me. When I wrench myself from her to go to the study, it physically hurts.

By the time I'm finished on the phone with one police officer, then a detective, then the pilot for the private jet, Shae has dozed off with the lights on. In her bedroom, I check the French doors are locked and flick off the lamps. If I slipped into bed beside her, we would make love all night. But I have a plane to catch. Having to pull myself away from her for the second time causes my stomach to ball up.

There isn't even time for a shower, and I head downstairs again.

"Sir. I took the liberty of packing you some food. I overheard Shae's family could be in danger. How long will you stay in Townsville?"

"I'm not sure. I've talked the detective into using me as bait because Brett's eluded them so far."

"Brett is in Townsville?"

"The police picked up that he's used his credit card there a few times."

"Which perhaps means the bloodied note isn't from him, unless he has an accomplice."

"He could've posted it, then flown up north. This time, they found a partial print on the note, Jamison. They went to his parents' house to take prints from his belongings. It's him, Jamison. Brett is doing this."

"I'm... shocked. I can't believe it."

"The detective doesn't like how Brett appeared to know about Shae's mom not being well when he last phoned. They're worried he's stalking Shae's family. Then there's the blood-spattered note, added to my suspicions around the sea glass which caused Dad's accident—a fact I just shared with them. If this is all true, Jamison, Brett might be… a killer."

"And you're leaving for Townsville to lure someone who's attempted to kill you once already." Jamison's gaze locks with mine. His mouth is a thin, tense line.

"I have to do this. He needs to be caught. The earlier I get there, the sooner I can bait him before he does something stupid."

"What shall I tell Miss Love?"

"Tell her I was called to Melbourne on business. We mustn't scare her. She won't mind my telling you, but she's getting some vision back—not 20-20 yet, but it's coming, Jamison. Take care of her while I go sort this Brett situation out. When I return, we can have a double celebration."

I'm flawed by the fact that Brett had tried to kill me, or at the very least, cause an extremely serious accident. *He killed my father instead.* Every time I think about it, my hands ball.

"I don't like this," Jamison says. "You're putting your life in extreme danger."

"There'll be undercover policemen around me. I don't have a choice."

I ignore Jamison's concerned expression and text Brett the message the detective advised me to send.

Brett. I'm in Townsville. Let's sort this out once and for all. Meet me at Romeo Café at eight.

SHAE

The next morning, Jamison tells me that Drew had to go on business to Melbourne for a day or two. Jamison seems upset though, and he's quieter than usual. That, coupled with the fact that I overhear a telephone conversation regarding a delay because someone didn't arrive at the meeting point, makes me wonder what's really going on. I conclude Lucas is up to something with his claim on Drew's inheritance.

Drew hadn't mentioned Lucas's threat much. He probably didn't want to burden me. I decide not to let it worry me, because I'd love Drew even if he was a pauper and that's not going to happen anyway.

Each day my eyesight improves. It means I'm more impatient to see Drew. On the third day he's away, I take a sneak peek at his bedroom. It's huge and masculine with its black, gray, and white color scheme, and the giant box bed. My insides heave sinfully at the thought of sleeping with Drew here.

I wander farther into his room and inspect the view. Boomer follows me and sniffs the air. He seems unsettled. Maybe he misses Drew. They're firm friends. Boomer must sense the wanna-be-vet in Drew. There are several security men dressed in navy and light blue uniforms on the grounds. I wasn't aware of them until my vision returned. They had certainly remained discreet but seeing them unnerves me. They resemble policemen and I wonder if they watch me while I swim or sunbathe. I had hesitated over shutting the French doors last night as per Drew's request, but I decided there's enough security around the property for it to be safe to leave the second-floor door open. Drew's acting over-protective.

It's liberating to finally see the clothes I wear each day. I decide on a bikini and yellow sundress today. It reflects my happy mood and even though I don't usually wear dresses, it's a shame not to give it an airing when Jamison went to so much trouble choosing outfits for me.

On my way to breakfast, I find myself still counting paces. Except, now I can witness the cold marble floor change to a thick carpet, then to a plush rug. I see the big grandfather clock which tocks and the mantle clock which ticks and the chandelier that clinks in the wind in the White Room. And when I went to visit *Sassy* yesterday, the sight of her unhooked my heart from its place in my chest and it seemed to gape wide open like a swinging gate. I had stroked her hull, ripples of hope fluttering through me.

I pick up the newspaper that's routinely laid on the dining room table, but the words are black squiggles on the page. *Not quite there, then.*

I text Drew, having adjusted the size of the font on my phone.

Seeing blurry color today. Still can't read.

His response comes a few minutes later.

Wish I was there to celebrate. You should go sailing with Colbie to pass the time. We need to celebrate your birthday, too.

It's hard to believe I'll be twenty-five in a few days. I recall this time last year, spending my birthday alone on *Sassy Jam*, half mad with loneliness, half dead with exhaustion, running from the police, but worst of all, Drew hadn't awoken my heart yet.

"Let's go sailing, Boomer," I say, thrilling at his beautiful face and large brown eyes before he turns in the direction of the jetty.

Colbie comes over to sail with me the next day. She's astounded I've solo-sailed without 20/20 vision, although my colors are getting sharper and apart from reading, my sight is nearly normal.

Jamison packs us a picnic and we spend a couple of hours on *Sassy*, then anchor off Manly Beach for lunch. We use the dinghy and carry the cooler bag and towels over to the shore. She tells me about her latest conquest.

"He resembles Leo DiCaprio—except taller. Boy, can he friggin' kiss!" The slightly blurry image of her swigs on her water.

"Apparently you and Finn hooked up?"

"Nice brother you have there. Good hands."

"Stop, please. I don't want to know."

"How are you and Drew?" My gaze scatters out to sea and I take in the contrasting blues of the ocean against a lighter shade of sky then the green contours of the land. But it's like looking through a fine mist.

"We're fine. Really good." At least, we were until he left rather abruptly.

"If you could have heard the way he talked about you—I can only dream of a guy who's that crazy about me."

I don't mention how I've decided to try to adapt to his way of life, even if I'm not sure I can yet. "I'm going for a dip to cool off, you?"

"Sure." She finishes pouring champagne into a plastic wine flute and passes it to me. "We can take our drinks."

We wander into the water, still cold this time of year, and

gasp and scream as we race to be the first to submerge. Once in, Colbie necks her drink. "To stay warm."

I copy her, but it doesn't reach even a smidge of the numbness in every limb. We dash out of the small waves, diving onto our towels to capture the sunshine on our skin.

It's when I'm propped on my elbows, sipping a water and absently gazing at the scenery, that I recognize him. He's let his beard grow, so he looks older, but it's definitely Brett. He's at the beach bar ahead of us, and he has the gall to return my stare.

I pull my T-shirt on over my bikini top, but I don't take my eyes off him. "I think Brett's following me. How could he know we were here—"

"Where is he?" Colbie asks and sits upright. "What does he look like? I've only ever heard about the bastard. Is he the hunk of dark hotness over there?"

Realizing we've spotted him, Brett turns away.

"He won't know I've regained my vision enough to bust him watching me." That's why he was openly staring.

I stand, furious, and stride through the sand toward the bar.

He glances at me sideways.

"Brett. What the hell are you doing here? Are you following me?"

His face melts into a wide smile. "Shae. Fancy seeing you—"

"Don't try to sweet-talk me. You were staring at me a moment ago."

Colbie comes up behind me.

"Your sight has returned, then," he states. "You ought to give the papers that hot morsel of news. I'm sure the world will be happy for you. May I buy you both a drink to celebrate?"

"Why are you here?" I demand.

"Can't a man have a drink at a bar?" He reaches past me

and Colbie accepts his handshake. "I'm Brett. And you are a whole heaping pot of gorgeousness." Brett scans over Colbie's swimmer's body, her orange G-string not leaving much to the imagination.

"Eyes off, boy. I love a bad boy, but even you're a little too bad for me. Come, Shae, let's go." She takes my wrist and tugs.

"Wait." Brett clasps my other wrist. "Have a drink with me? For old time's sake."

I point with my chin at the beer in front of him. "You're drinking again?"

"Sometimes, but not to excess. You'd be proud."

I pull away but Brett's grip tightens. The wind flogs my hair behind me, and he lets me go and captures it instead, rolling it around his fist so I'm bound to him. "It's as long as the day I first met you," he says.

I try to jerk free, but he tugs me back. "Let my hair go," I demand.

"You're not acting very friendly."

Colbie appears on the other side of Brett and smacks his arm. "Last I heard, you two were no longer friends."

Brett leers and with his free hand, he pulls at the string on Colbie's bikini. Her top slips, baring her breasts. She doesn't cover up, but fists the front of his T-shirt, and simply smirks at him. "Unleash Shae or I'll unleash my karate skills all over you, *buddy*."

"If you're not going to play nice…" He opens his fist and lets my hair unravel. When he stands, he towers over us, bear-like in both size and nature, and today it's grizzly bear Brett. He swigs the last of his beer, ogling Colbie as she reties her bikini. "'Til next time, Gotta Go Girl," he says and saunters toward the road.

BRETT

Shae's sight has returned. How unexpected. I must change my plans. With Drew nicely removed to Townsville, I had decided to take what I wanted tonight. Watching Shae stretch out on the beach, her bikini barely covering her breasts and muff, the urge to have her flooded through me. It was an unstoppable avalanching river of fire, one that couldn't be put out without tweaking those pert nipples and biting down on them while plunging myself into her and seeing her eyes pop with my power.

Before I knew she was no longer blind, the voice in my head told me I could go to her room tonight because she can't see me anyway. I'm tired of waiting for her. This game is taking too long. I'd made the plan to enter through the French doors as usual, lock her bedroom door from the inside, and take her for myself. Drew's conveniently away. No one would overhear us. I'd be gone before she could blindly stumble downstairs to fetch Jamison. How could she know who it was? Then I could continue with my long-term scheme to have her fall in love with me.

But now she can see again, and I mustn't visit her room anymore.

As Shae and Colbie return to their dinghy, desire swells and throbs through me. Having her near, her hair wrapped around my hand... I need to bring forward my long game plan.

My phone pings with a notification telling me Drew has landed in Sydney. I'd downloaded a tracker app to both their phones during one of my nocturnal visits. He's given up on meeting me in Townsville, then. Did he think I was so dumb as to be baited? The only person doing any baiting here is me.

But I'm sick of this love triangle. Seeing Shae today—smelling her, touching her hair—has made me impatient. Three's too many of us for one relationship. One of us must go, and it's not going to be me.

Patience isn't my strong point, but I force myself to wait until I know where Drew goes from the airport. He doesn't return home to the lovely Shae, but I track him to *Vega HQ*. How could he put work before Shae? I would never do that to her.

I head toward his office and park on the side of the road. Security is high here, so I plan to proceed on foot and head him off in the underground parking lot. I pull my hoodie on to hide my face from security cameras and tuck the kitchen knife I'd stolen into the pocket. I'll avoid getting filmed attacking him on CCTV, but the weapon should force him into my car and he can drive us out of here. No cops. No record of me. Then when we're somewhere quiet, I'll enjoy watching the life drain from his eyes—finally. No more love triangle.

When I spot Drew getting out by the front of the building, I realize he's caught a taxi from the airport rather than use his chauffeur. I fast march toward him, only three cars ahead of mine. *Even better.* But as I'm approaching Drew, a tall man in a suit greets him. I dive behind a nearby post box and crouch.

"I've been told what's happening," the suit says. "Gavin briefed me after the police interviewed me. I needed to assure you I have nothing to do with this. I came on a bit strong when we first met, but I was being defensive. I should apologize for that. I shouldn't have said what I did about Anthony. From what I've heard, you're a good man, too, and... and I'd appreciate it if we could be friends. So, I'd like to know if there's anything I can do to help with this threat, especially since he's my blood."

Drew considers the guy then smiles. "You're not responsible for what he does. Shall we go to the *Birdcage* and talk over a drink?"

They amble across the road to a restaurant and I curse them both. The feeling that I need to find out what's going on overwhelms me. Who is the guy, and why is he involved with the police? Is this something to do with me? Maybe Shae reported me after the beach meet up today. I let them go ahead and decide if I buy a baseball hat, that and my beard will be enough of a disguise to allow me to eavesdrop on their conversation.

Feeling dumb in a hat with a koala on the front, I'm grateful the bar they've settled in is dark and that I'm wearing black jeans and a dark shirt. I sit in a booth with my back to them, just as Drew's telling the story about how his father died.

That was meant to be you, not your father.

"And you were thrust into the media spotlight overnight," the suit says.

"I was. My father hadn't yet taught me what I needed to know, and it was a tough transition—still is."

"I'm here to help in any way I can. I know I came on strong before when I came to your house, but... well, I was on the backfoot and that's not somewhere I'm good at being. But put yourself in my shoes. I've had to fight to be heard and taken seriously for months, and I arrived at your home ready for another battle. I sincerely apologize. I deserved every word your fearless friend said to me."

"She's become more than a friend. I'm going to marry that amazing woman if it's the last thing I do." They both chuckle and I want to vomit. I crush the beer mat in my hand.

"I'd be happy to take you up on your offer to help," Drew continues. "I've seen you in action and read over your proposals with Gavin and—well, you make a lot of sense. My father would approve of you being a part of the company he built."

"I *am* sorry I never met him. I'm sorry it took his death for us to meet, too."

"It's never too late to welcome you to the family—and the business. I have a proposition for you, in fact. One that could make sense for both of our careers."

Sick of this mutual admiration-fest, I leave them in the bar before I do actually vomit.

SHAE

D rew is back from his business trip and my eyesight is almost a hundred percent. I wait for him in the White Room, aware it's the first time I'll *see* him—other than the blur four days ago—in three months. I'm impatient to drown in his eyes, to let them paint me with sunshine. I'm fidgety and walk onto the deck, ear buds in, to finish my audio book. Soon, I'll read again.

Boomer sits at my feet, as usual. Below, the yachts jostle on their moorings, and I observe people motoring in and out and enjoy the last of the day's sunrays on my skin. Maybe Drew and I can go sailing on *Sassy* tomorrow.

A strong pair of arms wrap themselves around me. The scent of fresh limes fills my nostrils.

"Aren't you a beautiful sight to come home to," Drew growls.

My body has been jump-started after a long winter in the garage and it purrs with anticipation. I rotate inside his embrace and a dazzling smile rushes to his lips. He picks me up and swings me around. I laugh and when he releases me, he maps my face with serious steel-blue eyes. My legs become fluttering ribbons.

"You can see me clearly?" he asks.

I nod and his expression jams with happiness. He kisses me, a short one. "I'm home and I'm not going anywhere." This time he kisses my mouth open, crushing my body to his. I decide then and there not to tell him about bumping into Brett until tomorrow. Tonight, is about us.

Our kiss becomes more heated and just when I want to take off his suit jacket, he scoops me up in his arms and carries me into the hall. "I have something special to show you," he says.

Jamison emerges from the kitchen. On observing us, he spins on his heels back behind the padded door, making me giggle.

Upstairs, instead of turning left to his or my suite, Drew goes right and walks along a corridor to a door which has always remained closed. He puts me down before standing aside for me to go in. It's a spectacular space because of the huge circular bed in its center, and the wall of windows that curve around the room and overlook an incredible harbor view and *Sassy Jam*. A fire dances in a hearth big enough for a family of four to sit inside. But the feature grabbing my attention is the round skylight above the bed, bigger than the bed itself.

"For stargazing," Drew says. "The room has always reminded me of a donut, with the circular window as the hole in the middle. When I was little, I'd cuddle with my mom and we'd gaze at the stars and sometimes the lightning before bedtime. Back then, I didn't know what each star was called."

"This was your mom and dad's room then?" I walk farther in. "Wow. Who lit the fire?" The flickering light creates shadows on the walls.

"Jamison." Drew guides me over to the bed. "I thought this could be our room." His eyes are hooded, and his words spark through me like electric shocks, making me instantly wet. He takes off his suit jacket, then moves onto the bed and rolls onto his back. He beckons to the space beside him and we lie down and map the blue and pink heavens—puffy clouds scud across the early evening sky like tumbleweed on a windy day.

"I wish we could stay in this moment forever," he says, lifting his hand to stroke my cheek. "No outside world. Just us."

"It's all I want, too."

He rolls onto his side and kisses me softly. I push my fingers through his hair and his tongue becomes more demanding. I'm wondering how to remove his shirt and tie when he chuckles into my mouth and stands. He watches me as he undresses.

"I'm glad you only have those skimpy shorts and a tank top on," he says, his voice a rumble through a sexy grin. I begin to unbutton my shorts, but he says no. "I want to peel them off myself."

First, he reveals his body to me, one item of clothing at a time. When he removes his boxers, he's long and hard and my body tightens with anticipation. He climbs next to me, immediately slipping the string of my tank top from my shoulder and capturing the skin there with a kiss.

"We've had so many lost chances," he says between light kisses across my neck, "and times when I've let you slip away." I'm adrift in sensation when he nips my ear and slides my tank top down, exposing my breasts. His fingers find a nipple. "Since the day I met you, we've been apart for most of the time, and it's felt as if I'm hurtling through a black hole. Or like I'm holding my breath." He shifts his mouth to my other breast so both nipples are pinched and nipped. "Then when you're here, when you're with me, there's enough air to breathe and the world makes sense again. You stop the hurtling."

He lifts his head to kiss my lips gently, lovingly, a palm

cupping my jaw. "All I need is right in front of me." Everything stops for a moment. The flock of emotions crossing his face surprises me; they flicker quickly and I can't name them all.

"I'm not going anywhere," I say. "No more running."

"I love you, Shae. I love you so much." His voice is raspy, his eyes flash with fire, sparks from a flint.

I capture his gaze. Those three little words hold so much hope. Like the three blossoms I'd seen when I was stranded in the doldrums. Or *thought* I had seen, before they vanished. But my love for Drew is not going to disappear.

"I love you," I say. "I love you, too."

He brushes his lips across mine in the soft way he does, the way that drives me crazy. I smile against them, repeating the three words against his lips.

His arms pulling me against him, his kisses are slow and tender, as if we have all the time in the world, and I guess we do. I try to control the rushing blood inside my body, keeping it at a heated simmer. Eventually, he moves onto his knees, tugging me with him, and unbuttons my shorts. He watches as he pushes them and my tank top all the way off, then my panties. He wraps himself around me again, bending to caress my lips lightly. His hips and hard-on rub against my belly while he strokes the crook of my back and across my thighs. My breath becomes rapid as I respond to his touch. I push against him. He kisses me more urgently, his one arm clamping me against his body as the other traces the side of my breasts, my waist, my hips, my butt.

"Did I ever tell you that when I draw a woman, I see all the scoops of flesh and they produce the framework of the drawing?" Drew's question breaks the heated hush between us. He skims the scoop of my waist. "So, I have a thing for scoops of flesh." His voice is low and husky as he comically raises his eyebrows up and down. The firelight from the bedroom fire dances over his features.

I laugh. "It sounds cannibalistic."

"When I hear it out loud, you're right, it does." He settles back, pulling me with him, but props himself on an elbow. "Let me show you instead." He browses a knuckle along my neck from behind my ear and his finger circles the top of my shoulder then slides to my collar bone. He's lost in thought while my heated skin leaps to attention.

"This is one of my favorites—from your shoulder. See how my fingers descend to your clavicle. This hollow is a scoop of flesh, like the concave of a spoon." I home in on his lips as he speaks and long to kiss them. "The most obvious one is the scoop along the curve of a woman's hips from the rib cage into the waist and out again to the hips." His palm scoops down the side of my body to illustrate, grazing my breast. My nipple puckers. "Or the neck—as it joins the collar bone, that's another obvious hollow." He shows me with his fingertips then kisses it. Next, he fits his thumb into the dent at the base of my throat. "This is the smallest one." He kisses me there.

"You've already checked, have you?"

"Yeah. I've already checked." Our eyes map each other's faces and the pulse deepens between my legs.

He lifts my leg and pushes a balled fist in the scoop behind my knee. A rush of cool air reaches my exposed sex. "Behind the knee is another one." Then he brings my foot to his lips as he kisses my ankle bone, right over the sea eagle tattoo. His thumb strokes the curve of my ankle, then under my foot at the arch, which he also kisses. My body thrums.

"But my personal favorites are near the ribs and belly. He sits more upright, places a hand on the edge of my rib cage. His fingers curl over them to my stomach. Then he uses a finger like a pencil to follow the line from the rim of my ribs to my belly button. He bends to kiss me in the nook. "And the hip bone." He circles my protruding hip, then carves along the scoop toward the silky hair between my legs. When his lips kiss the indent there, I gasp and rivulets of heat spray through my pelvis.

I shut my eyes and his mouth is on mine.

He's gentle and tender as we touch each other. Our bodies press together, and he replaces his lips on my mouth with a thumb that brushes along my bottom lip. "We could just carry on this way all night," he whispers.

I grasp his thumb and kiss the fleshy part of it. "If you don't make love to me right now, I might explode." His eyes widen and flicker with heat.

He reaches into the drawer beside him and fiddles with a foil wrapper.

Facing each other, my breath becomes thin and fast and when he captures my mouth again, I wrap a leg around his waist, opening to him. His fingers slide to their heated target, which is already throbbing and glossy with moisture. They dance in and out of me, flicking and sliding, his thumb always pressing and circling. He's maddeningly gentle so the build of orgasm is slow but intense. When I pull out of our kiss to grab air and groan, he rolls between my legs and thrusts inside of me.

I clasp him closer, whirlpooling in wave after wave of ecstasy as he drives deeper, and I'm gripping around him, pulsing without letting up. When my sex finally stops throbbing, and I can open my eyes again, he slows his pace; the world becomes our rhythmic breaths as we watch each other react to the sensations we're sharing. A crescendo of exquisite pleasure builds and takes my breath away. My eyes roll back as he plunges deeper until I'm throbbing in ongoing sets of bliss; reality recedes to the edges of my consciousness, and he is mine and I am his, lost in a people-less world on the other side of the sunset.

Afterward, we lie entwined on the bed, facing each other, the flickering of the fire the only light. There are no words; everything we have to say is in our eyes. After a while, Drew strokes my face and down my neck. I brush the skin along his shoulders. My body is soft and relaxed, like liquid mercury. The room has become somewhere without any concept of time.

"If I could draw, and I was drawing you," I say, sounding sleepy. "Is it all about angles rather than scoops?"

"Sounds right."

I trace the line of his cheekbone to his chin. "Like this one."

"You've checked my angles, have you?"

"I have." He curls his hand over mine, turns to kiss the inside of my palm, and then his mouth is kissing me again, hungrier and harder than before, his appetite for me awake once again.

We make love and talk all night. Neither of us waste a moment by sleeping. At some point, Drew fetches a cheese and fruit platter Jamison left for us in the fridge. We settle on the rug by the fire, never far from touching each other. We soon get distracted from the food and the cheese melts into liquid pools on the plate.

DREW

The sun is telling us to get up, but we ignore it and I lie naked, spooning Shae as she goes back to asleep. All I can think about is how one life with her is never going to be long enough. I still can't believe she finally told me she loves me. It meant so much, after everything.

We sleep until two in the afternoon and when we wake, Shae stretches next to me and I stroke her flat, smooth tummy. A bomb of desire discharges inside me and I could go again, but the brain part of me thinks it's time for a change of scenery. We should celebrate as today is Shae's birthday. Besides, we have all night. I force myself to take a cold shower instead.

When I come out with a towel around my hips, Shae, wrapped in a sheet, has opened the curtains and is staring into the horizon.

"Let's go eat lunch, or dinner, or whatever meal we should be consuming at this time of day, birthday girl," I say.

While she showers, I check my phone messages and emails. Jamison has called to confirm everything's fine, but the police haven't picked up Brett. They've diverted their search back to Sydney, though they have people searching for him in Townsville, too. It turns out the pieces of sea glass from Shae's bedroom are similar to the shiny gems which caused Dad's horse to refuse the jump. And Brett's fingerprints are all over them.

I put a security detail on Brody and Shae's mom's house, then text them to explain the media might swarm them when they find out Shae has regained her sight—which is also true. Then I begin to sketch Shae on a riverbank, my first drawing since I left Shae behind in Samoa.

When she emerges from the shower, I brush my lips over hers. "Happy?" I ask. She nods. "You want this? You want us? Even though it means living in Sydney rather than on *Sassy Jam?*"

"It doesn't have to be an either or. We can sail every weekend and take long holidays to travel the world on *Sassy*."

Not once does she hide behind her curtain of hair, which is softly pinned behind her ears.

"We can do that." I grin madly.

"And I want you. I want to marry you."

Seizing her, I laugh into her neck. "Five little words that mean as much as the three little words I never thought I'd hear. Wait here."

I go to my old bedroom to fetch the engagement ring. When I sit next to her on the bed again and open the box, she ponders it then me. "Happy birthday," I say.

Her eyes widen. "But how did you get it? I left it on *Ariel?*"

"Good question. It came in the mail. No note. But the envelope displayed your name as the sender."

"*Brett.* I think he went through my stuff. It's how he found your drawings."

"For months I believed *you* had sent it back."

She straddles my lap, letting the towel fall away, and kisses my lips. "That's the last time Brett will come between us," she says. "Ever."

WE ENTICE Jamison into the White Room by asking for a pot of tea for three, then invite him to have one himself. Once he has his tea, Shae tilts her hand to reveal the ring. With the teacup almost at his lips, he plonks it on the table and rises to his feet, speechless, smiling from ear to ear.

"Nothing to say, Jamison? That's a first," I quip, also standing.

He paces the room and makes for the balcony, but then spins on his heel and turns to me, his hand extended. Half-way, he changes his mind and targets Shae instead. She kisses his cheek. I slap him on the back. His huge grin splits his face in half. Then he hugs me as a father would. "My boy" and "So happy" are the only words he can utter.

SHAE

Something seismic has shifted for Drew and me. We're closer and more connected than ever before, like the space between us isn't air anymore but an extension of ourselves that's merely invisible.

Later, Drew and I cuddle together on the bed under the stars. We search the sky through the circular skylight, which acts as a giant porthole above us, naming constellations. We make love, slowly and gently, before sleeping deeply.

When I wake the next morning, I'm soaked in winter morning sunlight. Content, I roll over sleepily and fumble for Drew, but he's not there. I put on my T-shirt and go to my suite to find a robe. I expect he's in the White Room or having breakfast, but as I pass through the hall, I spot him in the study.

I stand between the open double doors. "Morning," I say.

He looks up, surprised, and beckons me in.

I walk across the plush carpet. "I've never seen you in here before."

"I needed to catch up on some urgent work and I went to the desk in my… old room. It felt wrong. Like I don't belong there anymore." He stands and circles the huge desk to fold his arms around me. "The walls in here used to push in on me, but today, it's as if they've fallen away. Everything feels right. That's what you've done for me." He strokes my hair as I lay my head against his chest.

"I understand what you mean." I stoop to stroke Boomer at Drew's feet. "I'm not aching to run off to sea and be alone. The spinning top that was my world when I wasn't sailing has finally stopped."

Drew lifts my chin and his eyes rake over my face. His kiss is sweet and soft and jam-packed full of love.

"I have something to tell you," he says after gradually breaking contact. He pulls out a chair and has me sit, then perches opposite me, his palms covering my knees. "I've made a big decision and I'm sure it's right because it feels good."

My heart stalls. The last time he made big decisions without me, it didn't turn out well. Boomer places his chin on my lap, and I cuddle him to me.

"I've decided to let Lucas buy me out of all but fifteen percent of my shares in *Vega Corp*. He'll take over the reins. I know it appears odd and sudden, but we've spoken a lot more. I've also seen him in action at the office, and he's the man for the job. And he's a Vega, my father's son."

"But he was horrible the night he came here."

"He apologized for his rudeness. He was nervous or defensive or something. He hopes to form a friendship, become a brother. A part of our family. I believe my father would welcome him into the family and he'd approve of my decision because it's the best thing for the company. Not only that, it's the best thing for me and us, Shae."

I'm too stunned to comment.

He reaches for my hand. "We can still live here, but we can have a different sort of life. I'll have some input on decisions within the business, but it won't be my daily job."

"This resembles King Edward and Mrs. Simpson when he

gave up the throne of England for her. I won't let you give up everything for me."

"I'm not giving up everything. Just some of it. I'm choosing a better life for us both. I'm putting the company into superior hands. It's not a sacrifice. I'm going to focus on the America's Cup. You should join me. The crew has already been selected, but the manager was asked to resign. We could manage the challenge together."

I whoop and stand. "That's a dream come true. I'd love it. Can I really?"

"You're free to do whatever you choose to do."

"But where does that leave you and this house and Jamison?"

"Even splitting Dad's personal assets with Lucas, we'll be wealthy. We'll continue to live here, and we can buy a fleet of *Sassy Jams* and sail the world. We could mount a non-stop around the world challenge. Well, it's what I'm planning to do. You can join me if you want to."

I play-punch him and Boomer barks excitedly.

SHAE

We roll through October and the weather is warming up, making sailing an even better way to pass the time while Drew finishes up at *Vega Corp*. Boomer always accompanies me and he's learning to be a great boat dog. Today, sunshine sparkles off *Sassy Jam* and the water like she's a glittering diamond in the middle of an ocean filled with twinkling jewels. The sun is a warm and thickset blanket on my back as I check *Sassy* over and get ready to set off.

At first, I sail across the harbor, never willing to miss the view of the Opera House and the iconic coat hanger bridge. But then I'm keen to hit the open sea and we glide toward the heads to find a spot of ocean where there's not a single boat or building, where my only companions are some far flying birds and a dolphin or two.

I witness the land recede behind us with excitement coursing through me. I work the winches to adjust the sails and pick up our pace but then tread on something hard. My bare foot stings. I bend to pick up the cockpit locker combination lock. It's clear it isn't broken. I'm a hundred percent certain I left it locked in place last time I sailed because I hadn't accessed it in weeks. The locker only contains a few of Drew's drawings—the ones I damaged and graphitised but can't seem to throw away, the companionway spare key, and Dad's gun.

I flip open the unsecured locker and search under the sketches. The key and the gun are gone. *I've been robbed.* But then why didn't they take anything from inside the cabin? *Maybe they did.* I slow us and heave to, throw down the anchor, and go below. I check for obvious things someone might steal—tools or instruments—and then I investigate the aft storage area. They could've stolen spare sails, lines, halyards, harnesses, sleeping bags… but nothing is missing.

I turn to return to the deck and a shriek leaps from my lips as I find myself staring into the whirling, dark eyes of Brett. He resembles something chewed up and spit out, a discarded hairball. His navy T-shirt is rumpled as if he's slept in it for a week, his uncut hair sticks up in all directions, his stubble is thick. He's blocking the way out, one foot in the head where he was probably hiding.

A streak of black dread slicks through me. "What the hell, Brett?"

He smirks, pleased with himself, holding the doorjamb with one hand, the bulkhead opposite with the other. There's no space for me to squeeze through. "Aren't you a sight for sore eyes, Shae Love? Or should I say… *Mrs. Vega-to-be?*"

His words wedge a shard of fear into my gut.

"What are you doing here, Brett?" I pull myself tall, taking in a breath as invisibly as possible. "Did you break in?"

"Didn't need to." His voice is smooth, rich chocolate. "I remember the locker combo."

The gun. I peer at his hands again, but they're empty.

He takes a step closer. "Where's my welcome hug?"

"You trespass on *Sassy*, hide on her, frighten the living daylights out of me, and now you're demanding a hug? Let me pass, Brett. I need to get *Sassy* going."

"I heard the anchor drop."

"I was… checking something. But I have to go home." Boomer whimpers on the deck. He hates descending the slippery stairs into the cabin. "The dog's getting anxious without me and Drew will be missing me. And… and the wind's due to pick up."

"Wind's *good* for a yacht, isn't it? It's early yet and Drew's at work. It's barely lunchtime. Let's go sailing."

"No, Brett, I won't go anywhere with you. Not after… everything. You lied, you broke me and Drew up. I can't trust you." I don't mention how George told me what he did, in case it angers him.

"What can I say? I'm in love with you, and a man can stoop to desperate measures to hang on to the girl he loves. Somewhere in that hard heart of yours you must be slightly flattered?"

"Flattered? You put me and Drew through the worst months of our lives—"

"Come on. We had a lot of fun. Disneyland, Vegas, long drives, and walks on the beach.

"Brett. Let me pass." I ram him, but he's a brick wall. I push against him again. He stands firm as if I'm a fairy and he's a giant. I'm reminded of when he attacked me in Samoa and how trying to run from him was futile. He's a huge bear-like guy. A fat slab of fear lodges into my gut.

"You're more beautiful in person than in your photos. Your photo has been all over the media. *The happy couple.*" He's not going to budge. I step back again, surreptitiously glancing around to find any sort of weapon if I need one.

"What's this about?" I soften my voice and try for a more friendly angle, remembering how I calmed him down before in Samoa. "What do you want?"

His gaze tears at mine. "I *want* to go sailing." His smirk twists on one side, eyes boring into me, his body stiff and ready for action.

"Do you need to talk? I'm happy to talk. Are you still dry? Do you need my help?"

"If I did need your help, would you give it?"

"Of course," I say and press a smile onto my lips. "What do you need my help with?"

"Easy. Sail us to Samoa."

"Us? You and me?"

His smirk fizzles. "Yes, you and me. Who else?" I jump slightly as he discharges the words. His face is pinched and spittle lands on my cheek. I wipe it, my anxiety stepping to a new level. I'm sick to my stomach.

"I can take you sailing, but not Samoa."

"Why not? You've done it before."

He's serious. I swallow my gulp. "It takes a lot of planning for a long trip—supplies, navigation charts, spare equipment, making sure the boat's ready for the battering. It's a four-week crossing. Plus, it's October, which is cyclone season. Another time though, yeah?"

"We can reach New Zealand and stock the boat, then get her fully prepared. You sailed to Samoa last year… almost exactly a year ago, wasn't it?" His gaze leaves me for the first time, and he skims the view through a porthole. "Those were the days—best days of my life." His head swings back to me and I shrink into myself when his eyes turn stormy.

"I… Things are… different," I say.

"How? Here's you and me on *Sassy Jam*. Let's go."

"I'm marrying Drew—"

"*No.* No, you're not." The words spew from his lips and he seizes my arms. "He's got enough. He can't have *you* as well. Grant me a little good in my life. I'm so alone in this world and no one fills that hole except you. We shared something special during our days in Samoa. You know it, you're just fighting it."

"You haven't met Lucas? Your half-brother. Don't you want to meet him? You're not alone at all."

"I don't have a half-brother."

"You do. He came to visit Drew. Your mother had a relationship with Anthony Vega a decade before she married your dad."

"So that's why Anthony and my father never got on." His grip loosens a little and he glares at the sky. "I always thought it was because Anthony convinced him to pay my ransom." His fingers dig into my arm as he returns his attention to me. "Don't mention my mother ever again. The bitch abandoned me." We're nose to nose as he snarls, "Why would I care about her bastard? If she hadn't left, my life would've been totally different."

My tongue waggles but there are no words.

He strokes my cheek. "Don't be afraid," he says. His finger advances down my neck and over my breast.

"Please don't," I say, my voice wobbling. "Please don't." His eyes cradle mine and I drop my gaze. He pulls me in for a fierce hug and I'm reminded how huge he is when his body envelops me. His breath is yeasty and sour. My arms hang limply by my side. I'm shaking against him, terror slicing through me. His big hand squeezes my chin, jerks me to face him. His mouth covers mine, angry and hot. I try to tug free but hurt my neck—his hold is too firm. His breath comes in waves as he forces my lips apart, his tongue a livid animal in my mouth. He shoves his thigh between my legs.

My anger blossoms and grows. *How dare he? He's not going to ruin me and Drew again.*

I put every ounce of energy into the shove I give him. He takes a step back. I push past him but before I reach the exit, he has my elbow in his grasp. There's nowhere to escape. Boomer barks wildly.

"We're going to New Zealand," he says. "Be a good girl and get us going—and don't think I won't realize if you don't. I know what the Opera House looks like."

I yank my arm and it hurts as he squeezes harder.

"I didn't want to do this, Shae, but you're not behaving. You leave me no choice." He reaches behind his back and pulls out a gun—Dad's gun. My eyeballs pulse in my skull as I pan from it to Brett. His expression is calm—he knows he's going to get his way.

He tugs me to him. His cheek is against my cheek. "Once we're there, we will recapture what we lost." He's been drinking, but how drunk is he? "We can pick up our friendship and you'll learn to love me. If we'd had more time in Samoa... you'll crave how my body will make yours sing. We'll have sex on the beaches, in the ocean, all over *Sassy*. I've dreamed of bending you over her helm and hearing you shout my name to the universe. We'll have that, Shae, and you will beg for me. You'll always crave more of me, and I'll forever give you everything I have. Picture it, lying naked on the sand, the sun warming your smooth skin. I'll take you places you'll never go with Drew." He nibbles my ear.

"Speaking of which, I never want to hear that man's name again. Mention his name, and I'll have to do something to force you to forget about him..." He leers suggestively. "Let's put our harnesses on. Can't have me 'falling' overboard, can we? And don't even think of jumping. You'd drown or be eaten by sharks before you could reach land."

"Rather that than spend a minute more with you."

A shattering white pain vibrates through my skull as he whips my cheek with the gun. I slump to my knees. Boomer confronts his fear and leaps into the cabin, barking and snarling. As Brett kicks at him, I pull Boomer close before Brett's foot can make contact.

"You can either choose to behave and we'll have a great time together as we did before," Brett thunders, "or you can fight this... but just know that I'll fight back harder. Okay?" He lifts my chin to force me to look him in the eyes, tears coursing down my cheeks.

He straps on a harness while I crouch in a useless huddle.

SHAE

When we get up on deck, I gulp in the fresh air between sobs. Boomer nuzzles my leg.

Brett attaches my harness to the boat and to himself, then ties Boomer up on the cabin roof. A new frisson of fear fires through me.

"Pull the anchor up," he demands, then follows me as I palm along the side of *Sassy*, my cheek throbbing. I scan the horizon and confirm we're alone. There's not a slither of land in sight. Even if I did unhook myself from Brett and swim for it, I'd have no idea which direction to aim for. I'd probably drown.

"Best to motor or sail?" Brett asks.

It occurs to me he hasn't a clue how to sail, which is something I must use to my advantage. I check around us and squint up at the sky as if I'm deciding what to do.

"Motor. You could steer while I plot our course." *Then I'll have a chance to radio for help.*

"I'm not leaving your side."

"Then we're not going anywhere. Drop the anchor. I have to plot a course or we'll end up in the South Pole."

Brett scours the ocean. He's nervous, possibly because of

215

our distance from land. Or of getting caught. "I'm not leaving your side."

I release the anchor again and he follows me into the cabin where I perch on the nav station seat. "When Drew finds out I haven't returned, he'll have Search and Rescue out in force."

Brett cuts to me. "Then you have to radio the SAR guys. Tell them you've decided to go on a little trip and that you're fine."

"Okay then," I say. They'll know something weird is going on if I report that information.

"But, Shae, I'll use this if you say anything is wrong." He waves the gun in my face and I retract my neck in fright.

I hold the radio to my mouth. Brett presses the weapon's butt against my temple.

"*Stop!*" he shouts. My ear squeaks. "They'll think it's odd. People wouldn't normally tell them they're changing routes, would they? That's more for flights." He slips his fingers into my pocket and pulls out my cell, the gun still against my head. "Message Drew. Tell him you have to go on another trip."

Tears crowd my eyes. *I can't do it to Drew again.*

"*Now*, Shae. Tell him you won't marry him."

I take the phone, trembling. I can barely see the letters to text.

Brett snatches it from me. "On second thought, I'd better do it." He taps out a message, one-handed and slow because his other hand is occupied with the gun, and he keeps looking up to watch me. We're also swaying and it's hard to keep balanced.

I can't marry you. Sorry. I'm going on another trip. Don't follow me.

"Can we go?" he growls, impatient.

"No." I picture Drew receiving the message. I turn away to hide my crumpling face. "I have to set up all the equipment and do my checks. There's no point rushing preparation. Crossing the Tasman is dangerous."

Brett's face drops, a small victory. He hovers as I sit at the nav table and pull out my charts, plot our course, pretend to program the autopilot, study the radar, set the AIS alarm. I work as slowly as possible.

"Talk me through what you're doing," he says after a while.

"I need to take some readings with this," I wave the sextant at him, "from on deck. It helps me navigate using the sun and stars." I don't reveal we have an autopilot because using the sextant will delay us.

"There are no stars," he says and throws his hand up to the blue sky.

"Why don't you allow me to do the sailing? You can do the crazy-dude-with-a-gun thing." I push past him to go up on deck and he follows, holding the harness that's connected to me.

"I'm not crazy," he states.

"Sure. Kidnapping me to sail across the Tasman without any equipment checks or supplies or food isn't crazy at all. If something happens and we run into a bad storm, we could die—either from capsizing or starvation."

He slumps onto the bench seat. "Let's go north first, then. We can get organized farther up the Australian coast."

"That'd be safer." I take more readings with the sextant. "I need the almanacs to finish this off." I jump below and write down some notes, check the books, scribble more notes. Brett reviews my every move, so close I keep banging his arm with mine.

"What are you doing?" he asks.

"I'm getting us set up. Does it look like I'm reaching for the radio to yell for help?"

"Now why would you do that? I'm not going to hurt you, Shae. I love you. I want us to be together. If I was going to harm you, I'd have done so already. I've sat by your side while you've slept, helpless, in your room at Drew's house—"

"You broke into Drew's?"

"Didn't need to. You left the French doors open for me. I took your actions as a secret invitation from your subconscious self—the part of you that loves me."

I'm horrified and speechless for a moment as I recall the times I thought Drew was in my room watching me. *It hadn't been Drew.* I'm about to tell Brett he cannot force me to love him, that I'll never love him, when I spot the EPIRB and an idea sparks.

George said he registered the EPIRB to Drew for his and Finn's journey from Samoa. I need enough time to set it off so emergency services will receive my distress call and location. *Will Brett bust me?* I flick some more switches, attempting to appear busy and as if I'm doing what needs to be done. When I lift the beacon from its bracket, I don't dare look at Brett. I raise the antennae and press the button in one movement.

Brett snatches it from me. "What's this? A radio?"

"No, it's an alarm," I lie. "It will sound if other ships are in the area, then we can adjust our course and avoid a collision." My voice quivers and my hands shake. "Can you put it in the bracket?"

He reaches behind me and does as I asked. "Are we ready to sail yet?"

"Nearly. I need to set the sails first. Like I said, there's no rushing things. Things can go wrong at sea quickly if you're not careful." I wind him up a bit, taking back a little power.

Half an hour later, I can't delay anymore, and we begin slicing through the waves, north toward Queensland. I helm *Sassy*, tacking back and forth and on the slowest route I can, even backward. Why hasn't someone arrived yet? We're not far off the coast. The EPIRB might not be working or the batteries are flat.

The AIS sounds sharply and I jump below to check the radar. There's a craft south of us and closing in. I wait to determine its course. It appears to be following us.

"What was the alarm for?" Brett is behind me again, both hands possessively on my hips. The hardness of him presses into my back.

"There's another boat but it's out west," I say, fighting to keep my voice composed. "It's not a problem for us on our current trajectory."

Sassy gets buffeted, and I jump on deck again and scour the ocean behind us. I take the helm and try to stay focussed.

Brett places his hand over mine—the one on the tiller. I must keep him calm and distracted so I avoid pulling away.

"Sit next to me." His voice is caramel smooth.

"I get better vision standing. It's safer."

"We could do our sunset ritual in the cockpit later. You have *some* food on board."

"Yeah." I plunder the horizon behind us and make out a silver speck. *They're catching us.* I divert *Sassy* out of the line of the wind to cause the sails to luff.

"Need to put in a reef," I say. It will reduce our speed further. He doesn't comprehend we could reach twenty knots if I was handling *Sassy* differently.

But then he sees the rapidly gaining speck.

He stands and squints at it, his hands cupped against the glaring sun. "Is that the boat you mentioned?"

I trace the surface of the ocean and hold my breath to control my reaction. It's gaining on us. "Guess so."

"Even I can work out that's south not west."

"Must've changed course. It is allowed."

After I've put in a reef, he sits and tracks the boat as it reduces the gap between us. After a few minutes, he jumps to his feet and latches onto my shoulder. "We need to go faster. What about the motor?"

"Okay. I have to furl the sails first, though."

He kicks out at the bench seat. "Can't you make this stupid boat move any quicker?"

I zap him with a sharp look. "It's not a Porsche, Brett."

"Faster," he demands, the cold barrel of the gun in the middle of my forehead, "or you don't live to see how this ends."

Trying not to shut my eyes, I say, "It's a police boat, Brett. They're going to catch us with their powerful motor. I sent an SOS message. They have my location. It's over. So far, you've done nothing that can't be put right. Don't make it worse for yourself. Put down the gun."

He shoves me backward. I stumble onto the bench seat and he raises the gun at me again. Boomer, suddenly free, races up the side of *Sassy* and snarls at Brett. Brett's clearly not capable of tying knots. But then he rushes at Boomer, pushing him overboard. I throw myself over the gunwale to reach Boomer but the distance to the water is too far and we're already leaving him behind. I work to unclip my harness. I'm still attached to Brett. I need to jump in after Boomer with a lifebuoy ring. Brett flings me aside.

"We have to turn around," I shriek and leap for the helm.

Brett grips my elbow. "We're not turning around."

"You cannot force me to love you, Brett. You cannot just take me. We could sail to the ends of this Earth and I'll still love Drew. If I never see him again for the rest of my life, I'll still be in love with him."

Brett's face contorts, this time with sorrow rather than anger.

Behind him, an unfamiliar craft is almost on us. It cuts its engine and drifts closer.

A megaphone screeches before a voice says, "Brett. Stop the boat."

I'd expected to be addressed by Search & Rescue men or the police, not by Drew. I hunt for him and find Drew standing next to Christian, his friend from Portsmouth.

Drew lifts a megaphone to his mouth. "Brett, we can work this out. Let me aboard." They're just meters away.

Two other vessels approach from behind them, one is a bright orange SAR boat. They would've notified Drew when I set off the beacon and was in trouble.

Brett grabs me, his arm a clamp that crushes me to him. The gun swipes past my nose as he widens his stance to keep balanced. I use my elbows to sharply shove him, but his grasp strengthens, and he puts the barrel to my head again. "Do as I say, and you'll be fine," he says between gritted teeth.

"Brett. Don't do this," I scream. "You could get hurt."

He chuckles. "It's only Drew. He wouldn't hurt a fly."

I have one arm free and lift it, elbowing Brett in the gut. At the same moment, Drew launches himself across the meter gap, attempting to board *Sassy*. Brett's face congeals with fury, and there's the swing of the gun and a sound that rips through my brain and gashes the silence.

Drew plunges into the ocean.

SHAE

"**N**o," I scream. "No, no, no." I scramble to the gunwale and lean over to search for Drew. He's floating and still taking in air, but the seawater is purple with blood and his eyes roll back in his head. I fight to unclip my harness from Brett, but he grips my wrists.

"What have you done?"

Brett flinches when I repeatedly kick at the same spot on his shin then wallop his face. He has a monster inside him—like my father and Connor had. *There's no taming it.*

"If you've killed him, then you can kill me, too."

I punch at him again as he drags me to the other side of *Sassy*, trying to hug me to him.

"He just wouldn't take the hint. Why couldn't he let us be? No one wants to be in a love triangle."

"We *aren't* in a love triangle. I have always loved Drew. Only Drew. He was your *best* friend, like a brother to you. You told me that. Help me save him. Let me go. Please, Brett."

Brett's mouth is open and contorted but he shakes his head no.

"You really are insane if you believe you'll get away with this." My voice is shrill with panic. "You're going to go to jail for the rest of your life. Every person here will testify against you."

His shoulders chug. "They locked me up and cut off my finger," he shouts. "I can't be locked up—" A sound resembling the wail of a thousand ghosts bursts from him. He climbs onto the gunwale and unclips his harness—not from me, but from *Sassy*. He turns to face me, then extends his arms resembling Jesus on the cross. His expression tears apart, and then he falls backward into the ocean. The harness snaps taut between us and drags me forward and over the side of the boat.

I bellyflop into the water.

Brett's gaze calmly pierces mine as he lets the air out of his lungs and allows himself to sink. The harness ties me to him and I sink, too. I reach to unlatch and free myself, but his hand clutches the clip. I pull frantically at his fingers, but except for his prosthetic—which pathetically floats away— his grip is firm.

He's taking me under with him.

My hair splays around me. It's useless to fight. His weight will drag me down like an anchor, no matter how much I kick and try to swim to the surface.

Sassy Jam's hull slowly recedes.

But then Brett lets me go.

He unclips his harness from mine.

I circle my arms to stop my descent.

Brett keeps eye contact. I can't stop watching him. It's as if I'm his last connection with the living world and I'm holding his hand but with my eyes as he slips farther away, becoming smaller, blurry, into the deep, dark of the ocean.

THE CEMETERY IS LOCATED on the edge of the cliffs near Bondi. If ghosts do exist, they have a spectacular view. I carry two bunches of flowers, their scent tickling my nose as I walk through the rows of headstones. Some are life-sized carved stone angels, others are simple tablets like crooked, gapped teeth in a row.

The sight of the ocean makes my head rush with the recollection of Brett slowly disappearing below me. The image will haunt me forever—the moment he chose to both die *and* let me go. Did he do it because he truly loved me? Was there a small piece of goodness left in his heart—the part of him who used to play imaginary games in the woods with Drew; the part of Brett that Drew turned to when his mother died? I guess we'll never know.

My mind shifts to the memory of Drew as they hauled his limp body from the bloodied sea—another image which will haunt me forever.

Today is the one-year anniversary of Anthony Vega's death. I walk toward his grave. It rises erect and tall next to Drew's mother's headstone—their simple gray marble gravestones don't reflect the wealth they accumulated.

Drew is already there, having asked for a private moment with his parents. He takes the flowers from me and steps forward to place one arrangement on his mom's, then his dad's grave. He walks stiffly—the gunshot wound in his shoulder still gives him pain. He has a scar there, one that resembles a circular sun with sunrays showering from it. He stays kneeling for a long time, his chin dipped to his chest. I wonder if he's thinking about Brett, too.

As I watch Drew, my heart bucks with love. I think of what we've survived to reach this point. It seems as if love will always find a way.

When he stands, he puts his good arm around me, and we trace over the graves. I shiver at the idea he almost had his name on a headstone right there, next to his dad. Boomer sniffs at the soil around the grave. A SAR guy had rescued him after the waves pushed him, still swimming strongly, closer to their boat.

Drew combs my face, his eyes welling with tenderness. I kiss him, pressing our lips together for a long time, breathing him in, finally at peace. When the kiss ends, we contemplate the graves again, arm in arm, and I listen to the sound of the crashing waves against the rocks below us.

"I loved Brett like he was my brother," Drew says. "How is it he despised me so much?"

"Love and hate are close companions. I used to both love and hate my father. Even Brett's desperate need for his father's love drove him to loathe his dad."

"As I loved my father yet could simultaneously hate him—when I was younger," Drew concludes. "I'm glad I got to know my dad better before he died. It means the time we wasted before doesn't matter as much." Drew's voice is a wistful ocean wind.

He raises my hand and kisses the shining ring there. Our wedding is next month, and Jamison was ridiculously happy when Drew asked him to be his best man. Lucas has agreed to act as usher after we shared a relaxed family dinner together.

"When you got the text that Brett made me send you… about not marrying you, what did you think?"

"This time I was certain it was Brett up to no good. Then the call from the SAR guys came in and… well, the rest is history."

Whatever Brett's reason for letting my harness free, I like to believe it was because of love—for either me or Drew.

"Love," I say. "It's the most complicated thing in the world. It can weaken or empower. Unite or separate. Wound us or heal us. It teaches us about life."

Drew kisses my temple, leaving his lips there as he whispers, "It teaches us about ourselves… and it's the hardest lesson to learn."

FINAL NOTE

I hope you enjoyed reading The Tide Series. More than anything, it would help this early-career author if you left a review for The Chilling Tide or any of the books in the series as it means I get to keep writing because more reviews mean more people will read my work.

PRAISE FOR BECOMING SIENNA

If you'd like to read more by T.M. Bashford you can read Becoming Sienna, the spin-off prequel to The Tide Series right now.

"I thought the ending was genius!" *Zoe Bentley, Avid Romance Reader*

"Bittersweet and definitely left me wanting more . . . This was a really interesting take on a stalker themed story." *Allyssa O'Brien, Goodreads Reviewer and Between the Spine Blog*

"I absolutely loved the storyline . . . we see growth in Sienna, and the gradual peeling back of her story with her sister Keely was masterfully done." *Laura Hockley, Romance Beta Reader*

"Visual, colorful and emotional . . . the story is captivating right from the start . . . once I started reading, I didn't want to put it down." *Author/Illustrator, Sandra Severgnini*

"The characters are so well developed that it could almost

pass as a true story. This has it all--self-doubt, determination, suspense, passion, and an unexpected twist." *Amazon reviewer*

"T.M. Bashford teases us through a story that will leave you questioning what we think is real." *BookBub Reviewer*

Three's a crowd, especially when one is a stalker...

Sienna Chase is having the worst day of her life—kicked out of her nursing program, dumped by her boyfriend, and to top it off, followed home by creepy Dr. Charles Allerton.

Flying back to her parents' home in Cape Cod to take stock of her life only serves to trigger the trauma of her sister's death twenty years earlier. Thank goodness for Blue Rafter, the boy she gave her first kiss to at the age of eight. He's all grown up and their chemistry is instant.

Except Dr. Allerton turns up, scaring her with frightening gifts and messages… but Sienna needs to figure out why she's hiding evidence to protect him.

The police don't take her seriously. Her parents think she's drinking too much to numb her memories. Her only ally is Blue... and he's trying to save her from herself. Until Dr. Allerton's final gift…

EXTRACT FROM BECOMING SIENNA

"What makes you think nursing is a good career choice for someone who faints at the sight of blood?" Arthur's thick brows furrow, reminding me of an owl.

I shift positions in the armchair opposite him, pressing myself deeper into the cushions. His tutorial room is flanked by three bookshelves that tower over us. Part of me wouldn't mind if one of them toppled and crushed me right then and there.

Silence tramples over a few more seconds.

"This is the third time, Sienna. I'm not sure we can find you any more work placements. I believe it's time for you to consider a different path."

"I'm already five years older than most of the others. Now you expect me to start again?"

"Not entirely. You've earned a year's worth of credits. You can talk to careers about how to transfer . . ."

No. I shut him out. The thought of deciding on another career choice is too stressful. What if I make the wrong decision again? I have a sneaky suspicion I'm not suited to the life of a student, either. Mom won't want to hear it, but I'm more of a free spirit; I *should* be good at art or drawing or music. Except I'm not.

"Thanks, Arthur." I stand, ready to dart out of his sunny office. The dust motes choke me when I add, "But I need to reflect on my next steps."

"Please, Sienna. Don't rush into anything. And I'm always here to talk."

I give him a stiff smile and jerked wave, yank open the heavy wooden door, and try not to slam it behind me. Oddly, I experience a flashback to the dog I loved as a girl. She died the day after my sixteenth birthday. She was white and fluffy and despite being a mongrel we rescued from the animal shelter, she always walked with her chin in the air. Which is why I named her Duchess. I used to find her when I needed a good cry. A sudden urge to go home—not to my student accommodation, but to my parents' home—tugs at me. It's funny how I couldn't wait to leave when I turned eighteen. After leaving school, I spent some years traveling and took odd jobs—temp admin work, bar work, retail roles, because I hadn't a clue what I wanted to do with my life. Mom and Dad prodded me every six months, and then came up with the nursing option. I had no idea that the sight of blood—lots of it, not just a cut finger—could make me faint.

To relieve an oncoming headache, I yank my ponytail out of its elastic and march down the corridor, afraid I'm going to cry and Arthur might come out and see me. Outside, I head for the bench under the English oaks. It's off the main path and doesn't attract passers-by. On the way across the neatly clipped lawn, I pull out my cell and call my boyfriend, David. When it goes to voicemail, I wonder about calling Mom and Dad but they moved back to America last year. With the time zone differences between there and England, they'll be asleep. There's no one else I want to talk to. Moving around from place to place and job to job tends to sever friendships, and the students I share accommodations with are younger than me. I'm more of a mother hen to them than a friend. Instead, I let the tears come, my face in my hands.

"Anything I can do to help?"

I brush at my cheeks before looking up and into the gaze of Dr. Allerton. He works at the medical clinic where I've completed the nursing placements. Despite being a doctor, he's a little socially awkward, but sweet. The kind of guy my parents would like.

"Dr. Allerton. What are you doing here?" I ask. "A bit out of your way?"

He brushes his long fingers through his dark auburn hair. "Please, call me Charles. I was visiting Professor Langton. He was one of my tutors a long time ago—and I saw you. You appeared upset." He indicates to the bench as if to ask for permission to sit beside me, but then he sits anyway, his butt perched on the edge. He stares straight ahead rather than at me when he adds, "This is a great spot for—" He doesn't finish. Instead, he clears his throat, strident.

I peek at his profile. If he wasn't so shy, he'd be a catch. His cheeks and jaw are deftly carved, his shoulders broad under a navy Ralph Lauren sweater. And I recall how his blue eyes are psychedelic.

"Not been a good day," I say. "Looks like I won't be back to the clinic."

"Did you faint again?"

"How did you know?"

His sideways glance is furtive, embarrassed. "Someone at the clinic mentioned it. I remember it happened before when you helped dress a wound. Not an easy thing to cure." On that occasion, Dr. Allerton—Charles—caught me before I fell to the floor.

"Not curable then?" Tears form a wad in my throat. "I didn't think so. That's the end of it then." I fold myself in two and can't stop myself from blubbering again. The heat of his hand on my back is enough for me to lean into him for a comfort hug. He lets me sob, then gradually embraces me until I'm crushed against his chest. He smells like coconut, which is odd considering we're in the city.

I keep saying, 'sorry,' but I can't stop crying. He rocks me, makes shushing noises, and assures me I can be cured. At least he's a doctor and has good bed-side manners.

"At times like this you need your parents," he says. It sounds a bit weird coming from a man who must be thirty-something. Maybe he lives with his mom. But in that moment, I miss my parents.

"They're back in America," I say, calming down. I extract myself from his bear hug. He shuffles a little farther from me. "Dad's job brought us to England thirteen years ago, but they missed Cape Cod and once I settled in at Portsmouth, they moved back."

"That's the east coast isn't it?"

My nose becomes runny. I sniff and search my pockets for tissues, even though I've never carried them with me. "A peninsula off Massachusetts. It is beautiful. I can't blame them."

"Why didn't you go with them?"

"I feel more English than American. I've lived here since I turned ten. And college is more accessible here, financially speaking." I certainly didn't stay because of my friends—they graduated and were busy with careers in London, Manchester, and overseas, leaving me behind in what they believe is the backward port city of Portsmouth.

"What will you do now?" he asks.

My sigh seems to come from the bottom of my soul and I sob-laugh. "I have no idea. The thought of a different degree . . . changing direction yet again . . ."

"Why not? I'm changing directions. I'm qualifying to be a surgeon."

I catch his gaze for a moment before he hides it by looking up into the oak tree.

"That's impressive." I slump against the back of the bench like a deflating pool toy. "But I'm anything but impressive."

He puts out a hand as if to touch me, but then changes his mind and withdraws it.

"Don't ever say that," he says. "Nursing isn't everything. You'll find something better. You possess amazing qualities."

To stop myself from asking him what qualities he believes I possess, I check my vibrating phone. David has texted me back.

Sorry I missed your call. In meetings today. Can we meet at Beckett's at 7? We need to talk.

I struggle to take a breath. *We need to talk.* I stuff the phone back into my handbag.

Cuffing at my tears, I mumble, "Looks like this day is going to get worse." Unfortunately, Charles still hears me.

"Everything happens for a reason." He passes me a pristine white handkerchief, similar to the one my grandfather always carried in his pocket. It's ironed and monogrammed with the letters *CWA*. I almost ask what the W stands for, but I can't chat anymore. I need to go home and let myself ugly cry as hard as I want to in the shower.

"It's okay," I say. "I might not see you again to give it back. But thanks . . . for listening."

My refusal is like a slap. He jerks his face away and searches the distant buildings.

CHAPTER 2

"I'm sorry it's come to this. But you must've realized we weren't working out." David's fringe flops over his eyes. I had once believed our matching dark brown hair would look great in wedding photos. He loads another forkful of fish into his mouth.

How can he eat at a time like this?

"Did you ever love me?" As soon as the words are out, I consider how pathetic I sound.

"It might be the age gap." He takes a sip of wine. I pick up my glass and gulp down half of it. "We're at different stages of our careers. I'm moving into management, and you're studying. You still live in student facilities . . ."

I'll take that as a no then.

Part of me wants to say he could've asked me to move in with him, but there's no point anymore. Clearly, he would've if he wanted me to. Clearly, he doesn't feel for me the same way I feel about him. Another wasted two years. Another tear in my heart.

He hadn't even given me the chance to tell him about fainting today and the subsequent pressure for me to quit my degree.

I drain my wine glass, screw up the white napkin from my lap, and dump it on my untouched spinach and feta ravioli. Angry words crowd my mouth, but I can't say even one of them. I reach down to pull off my high heels and curse the short skirt I put on to impress my now ex-boyfriend. It's safer to storm out of a public place in bare feet so I don't trip and further embarrass myself. I walk away and out of the restaurant, ignoring his unconvincing calls for me to wait.

Back in my bedroom, the sound of my flatmates laughing at re-runs of *The Inbetweeners* comes through the paper-thin walls. The only company I want is the bottle of wine I bought on the way home. Home? This place, living with people I didn't choose to live with, is not home. I inspect my messy, miniscule room—a single bed pushed up against the wall to make room for a desk and chair. I'm twenty-four and lost.

I turn up my playlist on Spotify to drown out the TV and laughter, and pick every breakup song I can find, sob-singing to Adele's "Someone Like You". The whole time I imagine the woman who will end up with David. How she'll take my place in his bed, at his breakfast bar, in the passenger seat of his car. How he'll forget about me and how these last two years will mean nothing to him. It's delicious self-torture and I cry myself dry.

And of course, that's when Mom decides to make her monthly call.

Except even though I know she'll be disappointed, I want to talk to her.

"Hey," I say, fake-cheerful.

"What's wrong?"

The concern in her voice sets me off again. I open my mouth to reply but a snuffle drops out instead. "Bad day."

"Honey, I'm sorry. What happened?"

I give her a quick summary, interspersed with hiccups and sniffles.

"Come visit us, honey. I'll transfer the money for a flight.

You can be back here in twelve hours. Take some time to consider the idea. The house we've bought has a granny flat at the bottom of the garden. They call it an in-law suite here. You can stay there. We're right by the beach. It'll be good for you."

The idea of going back to my childhood home settles in my mind like an old dog curling up by the fire. I don't recall much about my life before we moved to England. There were Cape Cod beaches and ice cream. A school where I didn't wear a uniform. A quaint town and some friends I lost touch with. Annie, Blue, Natalie . . . it's hard to remember their names. Suddenly, the idea of being there fits. To set the clock to zero. To start again somewhere fresh. The thought makes me want to bawl again. "I'm wasting my life going around in circles."

My phone beeps to signal my battery's about to run out. I reach for my handbag.

"That's called living, honey," Mom says. She ignores the beeps. "But we'll get together, the three of us, and help you onto the right path. Everything will be fine."

As I pull out the phone charger, a white cotton square with the monogram *CWA* drops onto my lap.

The next morning, Jasmine delightedly informs me how a friend of mine popped over after I went out last night. "He said he was a doctor and you were good friends. Did you cheat on David?" Her question is accompanied by a giggle rather than accusation. "He's hot. I wouldn't blame you."

Prickles of ice trip up and down my spine.

Charles came to where I live? He must've followed me. Or retrieved my address from the clinic. That's not right. Or maybe I'm paranoid and he simply likes me and spotted me coming home once. I've always quite liked him—from a distance. Maybe he's a total romantic and hopelessly sweet.

Except I'm not ready for another relationship. And I don't know what I'm doing with my life. It's for that reason I pick up the phone and book a flight to Boston.

CHAPTER 3

My flight arrives on a day Mom can't get out of a work meeting and Dad is on a week-long medical conference. Just before the plane pulls into the gate, she sends a text. **I've sent an old friend to pick you up. He'll be holding a nameboard.** I guess I had dropped my visit on her at the last moment.

I wish I'd cleaned my teeth, brushed my plane-sleep hair, and washed my makeup-smudged panda eyes because the guy grasping the cardboard with my name on it is a Chris Hemsworth younger brother lookalike. How is he an old friend of my mother's? He spots me and salute-waves. Mom probably showed him my photo. Too late to pop into the bathroom for a make-over, I run my tongue over fur-lined teeth before pressing on a big smile.

"Hi. I'm Sienna Chase." I put out my hand for a shake.

"I know who you are. You obviously don't recognize me." And with that, the guy scoops me into a hug.

When I pull back, I squint up at him, try to figure out how I'm meant to know him. There's something familiar there, but I can't place him.

"Don't tell me you forgot about me?" he says.

"It *has* been about fifteen years since I left Cape Cod."

He takes one of my cases and points at the door we're headed for. "I'm not sure if I want to tell you now. Might keep you guessing."

"Oh, come on. Would you have recognized me if my mom—"

"For sure." He glances down at me, and I mean *down*. I'm five-foot-four and he must be over six-foot. His eyes sparkle —yes, *sparkle*—with mischief.

I stare back and thumb through all the boys I knew before the age of ten. And it hits me like a gust of warm summer sea breeze.

"Blue."

"Thank God. This could've been awkward otherwise."

But if anything, the realization makes everything more awkward. *Blue.* My first kiss. In the sand dunes at the beach. He'd held both my hands and kissed me firmly on the lips. We were eight. His family moved to California a month later.

"You're back then," I say. *Lame.* "Didn't you get tall?" *And gorgeous.* The boy I remember was cute but bony, his hair more white-blond and his smile too big for his small face.

He uses the clicker to unlock a black truck. "Yep. Back. Same as you. And you *didn't* get tall. Still with the same dark long hair though. You always were like a little perfect doll. Okay to put both suitcases in the cargo bed? It's sunny."

I nod, wondering if that was a compliment or not. He lifts both cases into the back of the truck as if they're bean bags instead of the heavy cases filled with everything I own. Being in the cabin with him seems strange—as if this is a dream. Maybe I'm still asleep on the uncomfortable airline seat.

Blue grins at me and play-punches my arm. "This is great," he says.

Nope. Not a dream.

I take in the mini whirlwind of flutters inside my chest. I'm not sure if this is embarrassment or childish re-imaginings—he made my heart skip even back then. I hunt for something to say. "How is it my mom knows you well enough to send you to fetch me?"

"Apart from the fact that we live three houses apart, we work at the same place."

"At *The Seeing Eye*?"

"Yep. I'm one of the dog trainers. I started there soon after your mom received the el presidente position last year." I've worked there soon after your mom received the El Presidente position last year."

As he drives us toward my parents' new house, we catch up on where he went to college, what I've done to date, and laugh at the coincidence that we were both in Amsterdam at the same time three years ago. He was on holiday with mates, while I worked for an office temping agency. We even frequented the same bar, which became a fast favorite for the both of us.

"You're back for good?" he asks. We pull into a driveway with a Cape Cod-style home at the end of it. He turns off the engine.

"I'm not sure." I get out of the car and appraise my parents' new home with its steep gabled roof, dormers, multi-paned windows, and shutters. Very different to the Tudor house I spent my formative years in. The sound of the ocean is nearby, though I can't decide in which direction.

"Your mom said to make yourself at home. We can walk down the side of the house to the in-law suite. She gave instructions for you to get some sleep because she wants to talk all night."

I grab my backpack and follow Blue. He carries both my cases over the lawn. His arm muscles protrude. He's kept himself in good shape. Mom's mentioned that dog trainers need to be fit for their work. I pull my stare away and remind myself that I'm not here for a rebound romance.

We enter the in-law suite through the back-porch door. Inside, it's more of a cute one-bedroomed cottage, made of wood and sash windows, than a suite. Mom's left me a new phone, some snacks, and even a casserole in the fridge in case I'm hungry. I turn on the phone and find a text from her. **Welcome back, honey. See you tonight for long chats.**

Blue stands at the window, taking in the view. Through the tall pines, the waves nudge the beach, orienting me to the fact we're on the bay side of Cape Cod. We used to live on the other side where the ocean is rougher. When I come up behind Blue, he turns and smiles—a flash of white teeth and laughing azure eyes. My breath hitches.

"We should re-enact one of our days at the beach," he says.

Heat sweeps through my chest and the blush travels to my neck as I recall the kiss in the dunes and wonder if he does, too.

"How about Saturday?" he asks. "I need to go now. Work calls." He turns to leave, but his gaze lingers as if he's reluctant to leave.

"Sure," I say. "I'll check if Mom has plans first." And decide if I can handle hanging out with a guy who makes my insides wobble. I'm meant to be here to heal, not to dive into another heartbreak.

He stops at the door. "I've got your cell number. I'll call." He gives a casual wave and takes the three steps of the wooden porch in one go.

Way to set me up, Mom. Strange she didn't mention he works at *The Seeing Eye*.

I pick up the phone to search Google maps. I want to figure out where we are. Then I check my email. There are a few from the university about my leave of absence, and another from Jasmine stating that I forgot to pack my heater and would I mind if they used it? There's another from a Gmail address I don't recognize. *You left without saying good-bye?* At first, I assume it's from David and am touched, but he wouldn't have a Gmail address. When I read the three letters that sign off the email, I can't swallow the gulp that sticks in my throat. *CWA.*

ABOUT THE AUTHOR

T.M. Bashford is the author of both romantic suspense and young adult novels. First published by Pan Macmillan and Skyhorse Publishing in 2018, in order to go to more book launches, Taryn just moved from the beach to the city with a family that includes teen children and a highly-strung dog who loves cheese.

She's lived on four continents, meaning her job experience has been . . . interesting—an advertising sales rep, a ski chalet chef, a late-night news reader for the BBC, and the CEO of an internet company, but writing is her true love.

As if she doesn't have enough on her plate, she's about halfway through her PhD in Creative Writing while tutoring undergraduates. When she's not writing or teaching creative writing, she's training for triathlons in the hope they will compensate for the fact she spends ten hours a day sat on her tushie.

Learn more about Taryn at www.tmbashford.com or join thousands of readers and sign up for her monthly newsletter which includes bookish giveaways, bookish chat and next book release dates.

For more updates and books you can find T.M. Bashford on Facebook, Instagram and Goodreads and BookBub.

facebook.com/TMBashfordAuthor

instagram.com/t.m.bashford

bookbub.com/authors/t-m-bashford

ACKNOWLEDGMENTS

This book has to acknowledge my growing publishing team because without them the speed at which this trilogy released would not be possible. So, thank you to my meticulous beta readers, my swift and voracious advanced reader team, my compassionate reviews team, and my avid social media supporters who not only comment and like my posts, but share them too. You don't realize, I believe, just how important you are to the success of my books because it's one thing to write a book, it's quite another to ensure people find it. There are millions of books out there – without you, my books wouldn't be discovered.

Thank you! From the very tips of my toes, the bottom of my heart, and the ends of every hair on my head (and you know I have a *lot* of hair!).

'Til next time…

xxx